# Under
# the
# Small Lights

# Under the Small Lights

a novella

John Cotter

Miami University Press
Oxford, Ohio

Edited by David Schloss
Cover design by Madge Duffey
Cover image by Kirsten Lewis
Book design by Dana Leonard

Library of Congress Cataloging-in-Publication Data

Cotter, John, 1976-
 Under the small lights : a novella / by John Cotter ;
edited by David Schloss.
     p. cm.
 ISBN 978-1-4507-0091-7
 1. Young men--Fiction. 2. Walden Pond (Middlesex
County, Mass.)--Fiction. 3. Man-woman relation-
ships--Fiction. 4. Psychological fiction. I. Schloss,
David, 1944- II. Title.
 PS3603.O86848U63 2010
 813'.6--dc22
                                        2010001957

Printed on acid-free paper
in the United States of America

*"I often think that we're all mere composites of our favorite people's habits: the way we talk and gesture and laugh, how we comb our hair and walk."*

– August Kleinzahler, *Cutty, One Rock*

To S.D.

## July 4<sup>th</sup> 1997

CORINNA LEAFED HER FINGERS ALONG THE SUR-
face of the water like an actress playing languorous.
The fire pit we'd lit for breakfast may have still been
burning, but I couldn't see the flame, the backyard
was too bright. I heard the tall house next door
open its shutters, the only house we could see over
the high fence, a borderline mansion.

Her back to the sun, facedown on the blue float,
Corinna asked, "Is my husband there?" She untied
her suit.

"He's inside thinking," I said, "very hard about
lawnmowers."

Our friend Star said, "You mean Willy Loman?"
and settled back to rubbing lotion on her new tattoos. They were stars on either wrist, eponymous.

I watched Corinna hold her suit closed as she
turned around on the float. Two years ago, eighteen
and unmarried, she was thin like a dancer. Now
she'd smoothed. Her dark hair was still dry. Her
skin would be warm.

The sun came and went away.

It was near afternoon when Paul stepped out of
the house in a seersucker suit. He sold lawnmowers

that summer, driving farther in from the shoreline, toward split-levels and trim lawns.

"That's Dad's suit," Corinna said. Paul touched a lapel and winked at her. There was a live current between them. She waved her arm goodbye and he turned back and leaned over the edge of the pool to kiss her.

There was a trick I wanted to do and so I made for the fire pit. I wasn't sure which of the sticks had enough of a flame. There was lots of smoke, but I found one whose tip was going like a wick and I ran to the pool and lowered myself into the freezing water, keeping the twig raised and hot.

"Ladies and gentleman," I said, leaning back into the pool until I had to hold my breath and stare up through an inch of water.

According to my plan, the fire would douse when it hit the water and I'd make a joke out of "swallowing the flame." But I hadn't figured how hot the stick would be still and could barely hear Star shouting "stop! wait!" as I burned my mouth and coughed and sucked pool water, gagging.

"That was a little warm," I tried saying once most of the water was out of my throat. Corinna was laughing. Paul skipped into the house to crush me some ice and pour it over cold gin. I got out of the pool and rolled the drink in my sore mouth, flopped onto a moldy deck chair to dry off, dazed.

Paul waved and left for work with a saunter and a straight back.

An hour in the sun, then "Jack," Corinna shouted, "are you too hot?"

"Yeah, do you want to go inside?"

She took the untied strings and lifted the top half of her suit off her breasts. Arching up on the float and rolling the lower half down her legs, she splashed as though she'd capsize, and I wondered how a body so graceful could be unselfconsciously clumsy in the water. She kicked the wet suit into the grass by the pool. "If you're hot then come in."

She kicked the water with a pointed toe. She stretched her arms.

Star watched Corinna from the other side of the pool, then glanced up at me, unsure. I got up again, rolled down the drying boxer shorts I'd been swimming in, reached the old pool in two quick steps and splashed in. I swam from one end to the other until my muscles were used to the cold. Eventually, I paddled toward the center of the pool and hovered near Corinna's float. I sank under the water and swam beneath her, eyes closed.

"That book looks good," I said after I came up, wiped my eyes. "What's it about?"

The sun was too bright to see her well. I grabbed her feet to push the float.

"Some Old West thing. Bill gave it to me."

There was a small cloud. She turned and opened her eyes full.

"Star, take your clothes off and come in the water," she said.

"I don't want to."

"Take them off," I said, "we'll turn our heads."

Star glanced around the fenced-in yard as if to see who else might be watching, rose, laughed a little nervously, played it off as spontaneous. I turned away but looked back in time to see her hands cover her small breasts as she ran along the patch of wild grass onto the yellow tiles and splashed into the water feet first.

"Is it a book I can borrow? Bill's never mentioned it to me."

"After I read it." Corinna stretched her body, arms bent behind her head.

I sunk under, swam toward the corner of the pool, eventually coming up by some hibiscus flowers. The tall house pulled its blinds up. Corinna let her index finger touch her pubic hair, drawing straight down from the transparent filaments just below her belly, her eyes on me.

"Brown?" she asked, "Or red? Paul and I were talking about it the other night. He thinks it's red. I guess it's kinda both."

I narrowed the distance to reach her, raising my elbows onto the float.

"Brown. No."

I glanced at Star in a corner by the hot jet, and dried my hand on the warm edge of the float. Corinna watched me, moving her fingers lower.

"Are you guys going to do some kind of weird sexual thing?" Star shouted. "Let me know and I'll get out."

"Quiet. Jack's just answering a question."

Star pulled herself out of the pool and walked wet

into the house. I turned to watch her. A spell broke.

I grazed my flat palm over the top of the red-brown hair between Corinna's legs, enjoying the rough touch of it. Then I pushed back against the water toward the steps. I could hear what sounded like recorded jazz from the tall house as I climbed out, walked quickly to my towel and wrapped it over my shoulders, walked inside.

I pulled on my jeans in the old library, surrounded by shelves with either Buddhist or Hindu statues behind spider plants, along with silver-framed pictures of young Corinna. She looked distracted, running.

Paul's job selling lawnmowers was mostly to placate Corinna's mother, whose house the sudden couple was sharing. With the old man dead, she'd planned on selling the place, but she'd kept it once Paul and Corinna eloped to Florida, let their rents lapse. Before meeting Ronan of *Ronan's Mowers*, he'd been spending his days in the worn leather chair in here, wearing one of the dead patriarch's cardigans, figuring crosswords. Sometimes both he and Corinna would come to Boston and spend the night at my place. On the weekends, almost all of them, I came down.

Usually I'd sleep on the library couch and Paul would wake me up when he came downstairs. I'd scan the titles on the shelf while we smoked: *Life and Death in the Salt Marsh, A Packet of Zodiaks, Eastern Whispers*.

Paul would ease into his chair and philosophize

about starting work. But, "You don't want to wake people up," he'd explain. "You have to let them drink their coffee." He mimed a stolid burgher sipping, then noting a margin with pencil, "read their newspaper, then" he made as if to primp his mustache, adjust his fedora, "you saunter to the door…"

That afternoon I slept and read till Paul came home. It still wasn't dark. Corinna came into the library in the short cut-offs she'd been wearing all summer.

"Where's Star?"

"I don't know, smoking crack?"

Corinna didn't like Star's new friends.

There was a wine and gourmet supply shop down the end of Corinna's narrow street where she and Paul and I tried to locate the worst-smelling cheese. We made it a contest. Matrons and tan old men avoided staring as we scuttled around the place.

Corinna called me over secretively and put her arm around me only to snap a bundle of Munster Alsace into my nose. I tried to sneak up on Paul with the same wedge but he saw me coming and dodged me, nearly hurling himself into limburger. My fingers reeked, reminding me I'd touched something that came from an animal. I remembered where love pitched his temple.

Back at the house, Paul made us all a gin. He never quit pouring and Corinna and I kept pace as best we could. Corinna, tequila and cranberry juice, got restless, moody. I divided my time between humoring Paul in the library and running my finger along the edge of her neck in the kitchen.

*You've had too much to drink, Missus.*

*No, I've only had two…th…no more than four tequila juices. J'ices. Ju.*

Her cheeks got red and I convinced myself her lower lip moistened.

*You keep me around to kiss you in the kitchen? I'm the houseboy here, no?*

*No.*

Newly twenty-one, Paul stockpiled gin. We drank and ate, then gathered up the old fireworks Paul had found in the basement and walked out into the dark street.

The houses were close together and full of TV light. The doors all had white wooden plaques from the Rhode Island Historical society.

"Hanker Codwright," I intoned.

"Tinker Smith," Paul said, "Whoremonger."

"I used to think those were the names of the people who lived there now," Corinna said. "I thought I passed them on the street."

We passed the War of Independence monument, passed the big houses Corinna had stories about, which I'd forgotten and weren't interesting to begin with. The houses were quiet as cards, falling downhill toward the water.

When we reached the surf and climbed out to the middle of one of the long breakwaters, Paul took charge and set a bundle of Roman candles up between the boulders. He lit the fuses with Corinna's blue Zippo. It wasn't cold but I put my arm around Corinna anyway, pulled her in close and she let herself be pulled in.

I smelled her hair as Paul ran back at us, his hands up to his ears. Corinna's fingers tightened around my waist and he put his arms around both of us. We tensed for the boom.

Nothing. So we waited a little longer, gradually easing our grip. I stepped forward, feeling the stretched sheets of their bellies as I let go, hopped onto the big rock, the small rock, over the gap, up to where the rockets were stuck. I re-lit them and ran back, priding myself on how well my drunk legs hopped the trail. Back together, we saw them flare up then turn on us. Burning, they sent a blue streak straight our way. They hadn't been crooked wrong in the rock but the flare-up on take-off sent them looping, burning blue over gold. As we turned and streaked away I could hear Paul and Corinna panting in my ears. Then I was concentrating on my own running. By the time the flares went *bang* behind us, Corinna was ahead by twenty yards. I'd drifted off to the side of one of the warehouses. I knew all of our hearts must be pounding a fury but I could only feel my own.

# A Real Poet

"I DON'T KNOW HOW IT STARTED," I TOLD HER.
"We'd spent the whole day writing."

Corinna rolled her eyes. "And drinking?"

"Yeah." I grinned. "We took these pictures. I just
found them. See, there's Walden in the snow. But
from there…"

"Oh, yeah, because I've never seen what the two
of you look like when you're drunk."

Paul cleared his throat "Jack." He jerked his head
toward the hallway.

I threw the pictures in Corinna's lap and followed
Paul into the big house's nook of a kitchen. The
dumplings, laid in oil seconds before, were popping. Corinna's project was successful insofar as the
kitchen smelled like Chinese food.

Paul held up a wagging finger, sauntered to the
bar tray. Corinna's mother would balk at the idea
of a TV stand full of booze in her kitchen, but she
was away until Monday. Not speaking, barely moving, I told Paul I wanted a gin. We lived together
through college before he and Corinna happened.
I could tell him I wanted gin without opening my
mouth.

He winked and poured two. Plastic clack. We raised them to drink. Even though I loved Paul I didn't take him seriously. I couldn't imagine anyone did, but no one cared.

"I talked with Ronan the other day," he said. "I don't know if Corinna told you, but we were down at his beach house. Clambake."

"Oh yeah?"

Paul nodded. Like Bill, he'd be amazed at what Corinna didn't tell me.

"And we're all there, you know, the family." He meant Ronan's family, I guessed. "He took me in the house. The living room was the size of both these rooms." He gestured and nodded. "He took me around, showed me the bedroom. They have it in a kind of a loft, Egyptian linen."

He leaned a little closer, sipped Sapphire. "His living room…it's more of a library. He's got books and videos and a large selection," Paul narrowed his eyes, "of Navajo literature, books about…their blankets. He moved a Navajo blanket aside and showed me a trap door."

From the other room Corinna shouted, "Make sure the potstickers aren't burning!"

Paul motioned me closer. He licked his lips.

"There was a little safe in there," Paul's fingers giggled, "filled with money. Jack. Stacks of it."

The potstickers were burning, but when I tried to turn them over, they steamed and came apart.

"Um, lawnmower money?"

Paul nodded slow, vexed I was only half listening.

Then Corinna was there. I liked watching her thin hands work the cooking.

We ate by the swimming pool. Dishes steamed beside citronella candles. I sank a spoon in the vegetable fried rice.

"Is this our first dinner party?" Corinna broke the silence.

"You think we'll try two guests next time?"

"It's like juggling," I said. "You introduce two balls, then three."

"That's right," Corinna said. "Next we can have Bill and one of the girls he's fucking."

Paul shook his head as though it were funny.

"So," I said, little dumpling falling apart, "you guys are gonna just set up shop here?"

"We think it's a good idea to save up a little first."

"Paul had a really good week last week. Did you tell Jack how much you sold?"

They passed a smile. "One thousand dollars."

"Wow."

Paul shrugged. "Oh," he said, opening another bottle of his mother-in-law's Gewürztraminer. "I worked Shore Street today."

Corinna bounced in her seat. "Are you going to tell him…?" Their eyes met and his said *yes*. We had been the only people in the garden of the world, then I was east of Eden.

"I figure, why start somewhere else around here when here's where the money is."

"Well, yeah, but they have big lawns out there, out past the village." I tried to help.

He nodded, eyes shining. "Ronan said something the other day. He said it isn't the size of their lawn, it's the size of their wallet."

Corinna couldn't help herself: "Have you ever heard of a poet named…what is it? Jadewin? Um."

Paul grinned in degrees. "Charles Jodoin."

"Yeah yeah! Charles Jodoin?"

"Sure," I said, leaning back in the plastic chair like someone whose thing this was. "Mainstream. Rich. He comes from money." I hadn't read him. For all my bluster, I'd never even cracked Charles Jodoin's poetry — the lines were all too evenly-spaced and formal on the page.

"I went up to that big house on the corner," Paul said, "and reached out and rang the bell. Waited. Door opens and this older guy, good shape for fifty, says, 'We don't need any more appliances.'"

"Word got out?"

"Yeah." He rolls his eyes. "You walk down a street, people make up their minds. That's why Ronan says zig-zag…"

I glanced at Corinna as she consolidated the food onto a few plates, stacked the rest.

"Anyway, he and the other…he and the poet are clearly a couple and I think he had a good look at me…"

"In your suit, with your gray tie," Corinna said. "Have you seen his gray tie?"

"I have and it's very handsome."

"So I think my appearance may have helped," Paul laughed a little, "but either way he invited me upstairs. I climbed up, mahogany banister with, like, imperial-looking carvings, up to a second floor where…hardwood floors, bookcases everywhere with books you knew were worth…I mean, you've shown me books, but these were…something else. And this old guy was there…" He looked at Corinna.

"Mom knew who he was. My dad used to publish Charles Jodoin," she said proudly. "We have his first book in the library. Before he got famous."

"Have you met him?" Paul asked her.

"No, but I've been to his house, I think."

"So they tell me I can smoke in there, and I give them the talk, the one I showed you the other day. I could tell right away they weren't in the market, you just know. But they gave me a cup of tea, Russian Caravan. If you see it, buy it. David, he was the big one, sat down across from me. He had Greek cigarettes. Zodiaks."

He and Corinna passed a look I couldn't read.

"Charles. It was weird. He just leaned on the bookcase. He was wearing, like, a kimono and jogging pants. But you don't notice because he was…" Paul narrowed his eyes and nodded. "He's the real thing. He's a poet."

The garden where we sat was surrounded by a fence. You didn't notice the fence, because the garden was neglected and wild. Beyond that, the bay village. The hospital where Corinna and Star were born is a mile inland. The hospital where Paul and I were born is twenty miles further west, past the

Pequot reservation and a few towns made of VFW posts. I poured the rest of the bottle.

"They're very interesting. I talked to them about Greece. I guess they just sold a house there. They're going to be spending the winter in Florida instead, but they're having a party first, they do it every year."

"Oh, yeah! I've been to that," Corinna said. "Dad took me once, when I was little."

"Either way, I told them we'd just gotten married. In Florida, not far from where they're going to stay. And David thought that was pretty funny. I told him the whole story."

"What did Jodoin say?" I asked. "Did you tell him you were friends with the next great American poet?"

Paul laughed. "Anyway, he told me Corinna and I are welcome. He said this'll probably be the last one."

"Why?"

"He said they were too much trouble and he was getting old. Same reason he didn't want to buy a lawnmower. They hire someone to cut the grass."

I said, "You should have told him to buy one, keep it around, and make his gardener use it."

Paul grinned back. "That's exactly what I told him."

# Last Year

THE NIGHT SHE MET PAUL, WE ALL GOT DRUNK ON my couch, Corinna in between us. The orgy impulse can be something other than showing off. It can be the illusion of collective love.

That October morning before anything happened, she and I had walked thorough Chinatown. She didn't know Paul, had only heard me go on about him.

"Wasn't this the Combat Zone?"

"Before I got here. It's a shadow of its former self," I said, quoting a cab driver. Would I put my arm around her here? Or by the Copley fountain, where my recent girlfriend Emily and I had splashed each other the month before? "Emily and I said we wanted a tour of the combat zone, but he just squared a couple of blocks. She didn't even see one hooker."

"Fucking Emily," she said. "Fucking dirty cunt."

"Fucking Emily. We've got to hurry." The streets were filling with people leaving work, students in beautiful clothes. "Paul will be home."

"You have a friend who works?"

"Yeah, he got some kind of job. He won't tell me

what it is, he said, until he's sure he can keep it. Whatever, he probably just goes to a coffee shop in the morning and stays there."

"But wouldn't you see him there?"

On the one hand, I didn't care for how well she knew me. On the other, maybe I could surprise her, be someone new. I pretended to take in the Danker & Donohue garage and she changed the subject.

"Mom says we have to start thinking about selling the house."

"What! Sell it to me."

We turned off the last block of Newbury onto busy Mass Ave. This was the street I walked every day to buy a cup of coffee, read poetry, grow expansive.

"You just want my dad's library," she said. "Why don't we all go in for it together, and we can each pick a room to live in. You can have the library…"

"Paul can have the liquor cabinet," I said, wondering what she'd make of Paul.

"You can share it. Star can have the kitchen, so she can cook something for us. Not like she doesn't live there now."

"You can have the swimming pool," I told her, "if I can come visit."

"Thanks." She watched everyone who passed, looking for clues. "And the garden, so we can dry off."

We passed a couple of South Asian restaurants and an erotic cake shop.

"Remember!" she says, "that time we all bought vagina pops? And Emily was trying to lick it to turn you on…"

"Yeah," I said. "How about Bill, would he have a room?"

"Um, if he wants one. I just assume he'd rather be in New York, fucking models."

I turned to look at her, walking up my building's steps. She was still grinning — we'd both been grinning all day—but with mention of Bill, the high spirits had fallen out of it. Now we were reduced to gossip.

"He's coming up in a couple of weeks. We're going to write a play."

"Is he still with that girl?"

"Yeah," I said. "Have you met her?"

"No, but I called him—I really, I don't anymore—and she answered the phone. In his dorm room. And she was like, 'Oh, well, um, here he is.' It's like, Fuck you, bitch."

Paul heard our voices once we stepped out of the elevator and had a hand on the opened door when we rounded the corner. With his other hand he gave me a glass.

"Corinna, this is my ward, Paul. Paul, this is Beautiful."

Down the long hall inside, Paul made Corinna a vodka thing and said Star called and was on her way with some guy, they'd get here just after the debate started. He and Corinna talked about how they'd heard everything about each other and wasn't I great and clumsy and funny and stupid. I put some music on.

"Is this Tom Waits? No," Corinna says. "I like the one where he growls."

"Yeah," Paul said, "put in the one where he growls."

I picked.

"No, that's not the one…"

"So, Jack, is this where you, uh…with the lesbians?"

Paul shook his head. "Jack loves to tell that story."

"Yeah," I said, even though they'd both heard it, everyone had. Paul smiled patiently and Corinna watched him. She turned one of the dining chairs around to sit backwards, half her weight braced by her flat hands. I took the red leather sofa at the opposite end of the room. Paul separated himself from Corinna with the drinks table, which we'd orchestrated to look overfull, adding chips and a few packs of cigarettes and a slew of mixers along with the Jameson's bottles and gin.

"So where were you while this was going on?"

He shook his head. "I was at work. I work late sometimes."

"Is it three nights a week now?"

Paul nodded. I could see a couple of kids on the fire escape out the window to his right, working themselves and a case of beer out of the tight crawl.

"I'm a security guard at the Gardner Museum."

"Wow, a job." Corinna turned to me quick and her hair settled onto her shoulders. "Do you tell Jack what it's like, you know, to have a job?"

"I came home." Paul crossed his legs neatly. "And there was Jack in his room, in bed, the door wide open. Two girls, one of them on his computer, the other one," he set his eyes on Corinna, "fastening her bra from the back. And there's Jack, sound asleep, wearing this stupid shirt. It's…silk? With the word *Miami* on the back and a picture of a beach scene, a blue sky. Not just a picture, it's what we call flush…."

Corinna nodded and raised her finger. "I know that shirt! I know that shirt, Jack wore it one time when…I came over to your house when Emily had just left."

"I wear that shirt sometimes."

"She didn't talk to me."

The muffled shouts of the kids across the street grew loud, so Paul shut the window with a bang, which was the only way to shut it. Now it was turning dark outside, the blue gone rich — Star called it 80s blue — so he turned on the lights. The smoke in the room came out chokingly clear and the overhead fan that kicked on automatically with the lights started swirling it my way.

I turned around and stopped for a second like I always did to follow the line of smokestacks. Two years later I'd learn the whole Back Bay was built on marsh.

"One of those girls came by today," I said, tongue loose with gin. "She buzzed up. Her…the other one already told me the other day that she was 'intrigued.' She said, 'Are you *intrigued?*'"

"*Intrigued?*" Corinna bit her lip. "So she's Anaïs Nin?"

"Right, so. It was a bad day. I don't mean to get morbid or…I'd been at the…I don't know what happened but I'd been at class, then I went to the Café du Paris to have coffee and a sandwich. I was reading Beckett's poems."

"I saw that you had that," Paul said. "I was curious to read that."

"They're pretty grim." The buzzer jarred and I jerked to press *talk*.

"This is Bob Dole. Who's visiting?"

"Bob Dole."

"Really," Paul said, eyeing Corinna, "because of all people…"

I leaned on the buzzer. "Anyway I was real sad, like, heartbreak and worry and…she came in the door and said, 'Last time I saw you, you were naked.' Yeah, I know, right? Cute. So. I figured, alright we'll talk, and I made some tea." I started walking down the hall to unlock the door for Star and shouted, "And I told her everything about how I was bawling, and she was like, see you!"

"It's already unlocked!"

"Oh!"

"So, Jack!" Corinna yelled. She softened when I came back to the room. "When are you going to get a girlfriend?"

She was fixing a second drink, long fingers collecting the wet bottle caps.

"I don't know."

Facing me, she showed a thin mouth and a narrow chin. "Or how about a boyfriend, Jack?"

"Paul," I said as the door in the hall opened and Star hollered *Hello*. "Are you going somewhere soon?"

"We're HE-RE!"

I wheeled the small TV set around and Star introduced me to a short Spanish guy whose name I instantly forgot.

We fought about what to do with the TV and finally pulled it into the center of the room and gathered around the sofa. Bill Clinton was with us.

"Why isn't he saying *Bob Dole*?"

"There! I think I heard him!"

Corinna, on the floor in front of us, whipped her head around. "He said Bob Dole, everybody take a drink."

"Listen," I said, "shut up, listen everybody shut up, he's talking about smoking."

Star's date turned. "You be careful who you tell to shut up." His name sounded like Jock-something. The vowels were not familiar.

Paul liked fights. "I think you should…"

"Just. Everybody, I'm sorry Star," Corinna said, "but everyone please shut up."

*I was asked a technical question. Are they addictive? Maybe they—they probably are addictive. I don't know. I'm not a doctor.*

"Is he *kid*ding?" Corinna said. "I'm addicted right now. Of course they're addictive, look at me!" She fingered the cigarette out of Paul's mouth and took a puff.

"Time for something!" I said, wrenching myself up from where Star held me to one end of the couch. "Time for something I got here, a little something…"

I clopped down the hall, touching the wall for luck and turned the corner into my room — with its narrow bed and Navajo blanket, books and style guides, step ladder with a spotlight — black marker on the walls. I'd bought a bunch of sharpies one birthday and wanted everyone to write something.

Jack ~~Sucks~~ Rules!

> "There is nothing
> that man fears more
> than the touch of the
> unknown. He wants
> to see what is reaching
> toward him." –Canetti

There was a postcard from Bill on the surface of my desk. The picture side glowed with the New York skyline. The other side read:

> You know that shockwave of sadness
> that waits around the corner, under
> streets? It's been attacking. My new girl
> won't stop snorting. My secret girl is
> high. I stopped to vomit on the way
> home. I'm not drunk but I'm twisting.
> Art is dead. Winter in The City is
> frozen by the bite of car horns, wind.
> Heaven & Time,

Without hearing her come in, I felt the touch

of Corinna's arms around my waist for just long enough to notice her. She touched the back of my shoulder with her chin. My ear crackled warm.

"Whadda you got for us?"

I rubbed the back of her hand.

"I have tequila."

"Do you have salt?" She relaxed her warm cheek on my neck.

"It's in the kitchen."

"I'll find it!" She was halfway back to the living room. My own momentum wouldn't let me remember how her hands felt. Then I was already sitting next to her by the coffee table, feeling the dry drips on my fingers, burn on my tongue.

Paul kept intent on the TV, lips pursed. "Listen to him!"

I could barely hear what our president said over the static of applause.

*Would we be better off building that bridge to the future together, so we can all walk across it, or saying, "You can get across yourself"?*

Paul shook his head, sprinkled salt on the back of his hand. "I'd follow him into war."

Star's dude answered headshake for headshake. "Maybe not to war, though." He had a French accent.

Corinna's eyes were closed, like she was shaking something off. "Are you telling me," glaring, indignant, "that you wouldn't follow that…fucking man into war?"

"Nah." Jacques was warming to us. "I would follow nobody to war." He smiled like that was a good one.

"Oh, I wouldn't either." I spoke directly to the bottles on the table. "But if I were going to follow anyone…it'd be our commander…" Nobody was listening. I sprinkled some salt on the back of my hand and held it up for Corinna. She lipped it.

"Okay, he's a good president," she said. "But he's a deeply compromised man."

Paul's eyes were red. "*I'm* a deeply compromised man."

Corinna sucked on her fingers and ran them wet down the side of my neck. She took a pinch of salt from the table and rubbed it in.

"You guys," Star said. "They're talking on TV, and it's more interesting, at least to me, than your personal debate."

I inclined my neck and Corinna licked the salt off quick.

Paul and Star's date shook hands.

"Do you want a cigarette?"

"Oh, I don't smoke that shit, man."

Jacques stretched the word *man* way out.

"Forgive me," I murmured, "but you have a bit of a…where are you, actually, from?"

Star glared at me.

"I mean you sound French, but…"

"But…? Maybe I'm French. No. I'm just fucking with you."

Corinna and Paul had gone someplace. Getting limes or cigarettes.

"We're moving my car!" Shout and drag-slam.

Then Star was telling me my problem was I was too interested in where people were from, as opposed to who they are now. She said I liked to nail them down, define them against myself. Meanwhile, I fidgeted with the Cuervo label, pushing it up with my thumb tip until it revealed its underwhite. Skin.

"I'm from nowhere."

"You speak French?"

He smiled at Star. "Of course."

"La vie c'est ne pas merde, no?"

"You talk like Bill," Star said. "Like, the way you talk. Is that…because you picked it up from him?

"Um," I said. "Bill has a certain cadence, a way of being confident in himself I've tried to pick up."

"What do you mean, man?" her friend said, leaning forward, smiling. "You don't have to be…"

"That's weird." Star hadn't finished her first gin. "Just say what you want to say and be yourself."

I was happy to hear the door drag and to hear Corinna and Paul's footsteps together. "We need some music," she said. "Jack, turn the TV off. Bill Clinton won."

I shot to my feet, insisting we drink to our leader. "When I'm in love I'm drunk and when I'm drunk I'm drunk with love." Corinna fingered through my CDs before turning the radio up. She found a late 80s station. At least I thought it was late 80s until I heard "I Saw the Sign," but it turned out to be a promo spot. Then it switched to "Black Velvet."

As I wheeled the TV into a corner by the books, Corinna tugged Paul by his lapel into the center of the room. I couldn't have been sly if I wanted to, so I sidled over to join them with a lonely, showy move, flexing imagined muscles.

Like the show-off stripper who knows ballet, Corinna snapped her graceful limbs into liquid action. Unlike the stripper, there was no prep time. She danced more naturally than talking, she'd practiced alone.

I stepped behind her and pressed against her, hands on the base of her belly. Paul turned his back to her, and we danced that way, grinding, until one of us broke rhythm. It's hard with three people. Star piped up, chanting, "Four more years! Four more years!" We chanted and danced while Corinna climbed onto the table.

I navigated my focus to the bottle of Jameson's at the far end of the couch. Star and her boyfriend had disappeared, so I passed it to Corinna and then to Paul, who was also on the table by then. I fell back with the bottle. The kids across the way were still on their fire escape, probably doing soft confessions. It looked like they had plenty of beer left.

"Paul. *Paul.* Paul, go ask them for a beer. A beer. Yeah, have them throw one over here. *Here.*"

He slammed the window open.

"Hey! Can we have one of those?"

He cupped his hands, leaning halfway out. I heaved up and rushed over to grab him in case he fell.

A built kid in a red ball cap—a grin I could see across the alley—reached into the cardboard case for what looked like a Rolling Rock. He gripped it by the neck and spun it.

But there wasn't enough arm behind it, and it fell about a foot from Paul's hands and crashed in the alley with a light sound delay. Corinna laughed loud so we could hear her and the radio playing "Movin' Out."

The guy with the ball cap let his friend with the loose white tee try the hurl next time, and he pitched it so fast I could feel Paul flinch against the sill. The bottle smacked the edge of the brick wall, shattered.

I let go of his legs and staggered to the CDs. Cutting off the radio, I popped in Sibelius's violin concerto. It was Paul's favorite, and before I'd sat down next to Corinna he'd turned around, beginning to conduct the room with abbreviated sweeps. My hand found Corinna's hair, and I leaned in to her lips. She kissed me, full easy tongue, and I smelled Paul's cologne before I saw him on the other side of her, my palm on her legs up and down. She parted them, turned her head and kissed him, arching her belly up as his hand slid down. I eased down to the floor, fumbling with her big belt buckle. I couldn't see Paul's legs, he had kneeled on the seat of the couch.

I slid her jeans down and she lifted her legs up and out. She never shaved them, but her hair was blond and light and there was barely any of it. Her thighs were lean and strong. She parted them un-thinkingly and I sank my face down. In a moment, I wanted all of her at once and kissed up the length of her leg, loosening my belt.

She said something under her breath. It sounded like *no head room.*

"What?"

"I said I have to go to the bathroom."

She wrestled her way up, stood looking at the two of us. She gathered herself. Who's her model, I wondered, who's the person she's seen say something so similar she can say what she likes and be natural?

"Alright, go in the bedroom, both of you, and take your clothes off." Like a mother.

Paul and I crossed the hall behind her through the dark, smirking at one another. Once we got to my room I stripped the bed to avoid the confusion of sheets. Paul's jeans had come off already, so I slid my shirt over my head.

Corinna held herself half-naked in the doorway, light brown hair, and a short black sweater with a long, sloping neckline.

"Paul, take your shirt off. Jack, take your pants off."

She shrugged her sweater off and walked into the room. I didn't know how but we were all on the bed and my mouth was on her again. I could smell her thickly and I felt her breath go sharp.

# Bill Clinton Wins

"I'VE ALWAYS LOOKED TO WOMEN FOR COMFORT," Paul said, only just drunk enough to make slow sense. "My father has his own life. We talk, but it's like the way you'd talk to…it's just…you're the only man I can talk to. Don't…"

I answered slowly, pretending to be as drunk as he looked. Maybe I was.

"If you love me, Paul, you won't do it. You'll back off. Let me…"

He shook his head, past listening.

"Paul," I tried, "I don't think I've fully explained how much she shines for me. How you'll break my heart." I smiled at him, pleading. "You're gonna break my heart."

He grinned like he thought there was no one looking. "My mother and my aunt basically raised me. I played strong for them. My dad and I have a great relationship, but we don't talk." He angled his cigarette thoughtfully. "We talk about what's in the paper. Local news."

We were both tired. I lit a cigarette, filled my reluctant body with smoke. The night I slept alone on the couch, both of them in my bed, I'd felt as though I heard a procession going by, music, voices, and I wasn't a part of it, alone in a dusty apartment, a body awake and everything around it dead. I started begging him then. I'm still begging. Corinna was coming back up the next day, like she had in the weeks since she and Paul met, but unlike every other time, she wouldn't be coming to see the both of us. It would be the two of them in his bed alone, not all of us in mine.

"You don't even like her," I said. "What do you have in common anyway? She's…"

"Did you ever know her father?"

"I'm asking you as a friend, Paul. Please, if I've ever meant anything to you. Please let me have a try first, let me have some more time."

To Paul's small credit, he was in a position to say any number of things next. From You've Had Your Chance to She Doesn't Want You to Which Of Us Is Fucking Her to She's All I've Wanted to Don't Kid Yourself to You're Not Man Enough to You Think She Is Someone She Is Not to Why Should You Have Everything And I Have Nothing to She Chose Me Not You She Chose Me.

Instead, he went back to talking about his dad: how they used to sit soundlessly and watch television together. I remember the second time I met his dad and told the unsteady man that Paul spoke of him highly. Fading hair and unfocused eyes, he'd stared straight through me to the other side of the room.

"There's an understanding there," Paul said. "We

don't have to talk."

Paul looked at me square, hard but not angry. Then he focused not on me but around me, spaced.

"The first time I met her," I spoke slowly, "she was with Bill. And so she couldn't have been any more inaccessible to me. But you know, I kept thinking, why Bill and not me? I mean, we're basically the same." My last few sips overshot and the gin was ahead of me now.

"You're nothing the same," Paul said.

"She loves me, though. She's told you she loves me. And she fucks these other guys and I think, why not just call me? Because I think I'm pretty great. I'm smart, I like to read and drink…"

Paul stood up and walked to the sofa in three steps. He lay down and closed his eyes. It looked as though he wanted to put his hand behind his head but only made it as far as his forehead.

"I'm gonna put in some music," I said to no one.

# Two Weeks Later

"Not this song," Corinna waved her hand. "The one about the bugs and lizards underground.

"Jack is such a ladies' man," she went on. "Jack, have you told Paul about that time last year with the two girls?

"Jack!" She threw her thin arms around my neck. "We love you, don't we Paul?"

Paul poured another drink, the corner of his smile held a cigarette. He nodded.

She kissed my neck quick and danced into the center of the room.

Two and a half days later, they called drunk from Florida to tell me they'd been married someplace called the Bubble Room.

"Are you working on your television voice for when you go back?" I asked. Paul had been making noises last semester about switching his major from communications to TV journalism. Corinna and I thought he'd make a perfect newscaster. Later, he'd intimate that his money had run out. A string of failing classes had killed his scholarship. Marrying Corinna had been his best option. He said they used to sit up joking about it, until they quit laughing.

"And now," he launched into his joke newscaster routine, "the duckbilled platypus," in vibrato, angling his chin, "a mystery to scientists for generations, is, mercifully, extinct."

I laughed hard like I used to when he goofed off. Corinna seemed not to hear, poised, legs apart in her beautiful posture, staring into the alley out of the dark smudged window. I'd moved the couch to the far wall so she could dance.

"Your alley's really big, Jack."

"I've heard that."

Paul clucked.

"No, it reminds me of one of the streets in Paris."

"It kills me," I said, moving to the drinks table, "that you've been to Paris. As a kid. I went to Disney…"

"I don't remember it, though." She turned around. "It's mostly pictures that I kinda put memories together from. But I do remember my Dad coming down that street at the end of the day. We were staying in his friend's house. God! you would have loved the library! He tried to read me the stories, you know, but I wanted to read them myself. I couldn't, but I memorized everything so they thought I was doing it."

Paul chuckled behind me.

Corinna walked quickly to the CD player, happier than I'd seen her since Bill, and flipped through my CDs. "Where's the U2 I gave you?"

I reached around her and flipped the pages, nervous like always at being so close. Once it was playing she and I whipped ourselves around the room singing along to "Wild Horses." She took her shoes off and I did too, caught up.

"I'd like to walk into that alley without shoes on," I said, realizing how drunk I was, like you can be surprised by what year it is.

She pulled the heavy half-open window all the way up, wiping the dust off her fingers on those denim shorts that showed her legs full. I did her one better by walking over and lifting the screen up too. I only managed to shrug it up a little. Inching it, frustrated, I pulled it unset from the frame and yanked it down toward me and inside, setting the whole thing against a bookcase.

"Are you going to jump out?"

"Yes." I got on my knees and leaned. There was the low roof where the strangers next door held tiny barbecues. There were the spires of my old dorm, a converted palace from the gay 90s with plaster walls bisecting marble fireplaces. It was a low-rent rooming house only five years before I moved there. Just over my head—pressing my back against the frame, looking up—was the fire escape Paul and I climbed our first night here. Over the red bricks below, plastic garbage bags carried the light.

"Are you going to fuck that windowsill?" Paul asked as I looked up, dizzy again, in time to see him coming over from the drinks table, wrapping his arms around Corinna.

"I'm going," I said, feeling drunker then I'd guessed, "to walk."

Corinna tossed her hair back. If I hadn't been single-minded just then I would have stared at it.

"Are you going to run off into the night again?" She turned to Paul. "We used to get drunk up on this big rock in high school and Jack would start asking people who he was…remember that, Jack? And I'd tell him, you're Jack. Jack, who smokes Gauloises, Jack who wears cowboy boots."

"I asked one time."

"You kept asking." She reached her hands out. "*Who am I? Tell me really.*" She laughed for the story. "Bill would be flirting with Star or whatever he was doing and Star would be loving it and Jack would run off."

Next I knew, I was at the Mass Ave. foot of alley #902, still holding my empty gin glass. Barefoot, knowing they were watching from four stories up, I took off running toward the big oak growing by the dumpster. As I threw the glass, aiming for the oak but hitting the dumpster with a tin shatter, I shouted *Who am I.*

Upstairs again time seemed to have passed. Corinna'd shuffled to "One" and tried to sing it with me. The way she leaned in gave me the sense we'd sung it together in the past, but I wasn't sure when. Paul rolled his eyes in sympathy. I lost my role.

I did start singing, though, at the part where love was a temple. The instant she looked up at Paul he gingerly put his cigarette on the edge of the kitchen sink and poured a wineglass full of tapwater. Turning on his heel a little slow, he wandered down to the front door and left it open.

Corinna lifted herself from the red couch and leaned over the bare window. When I heard his foot-clicks in the alley I leaned out next to her. He shouted "Corinna!" and smashed his glass against the side of a car.

# Bill's Girl

*SHE'S SO INTELLIGENT*, I TOLD BILL ON THE TELE-phone. He'd called me from a new girl's house when she was at work, a bartender he'd met on Long Island. I'd been trying to get a hold of him for a few days and he explained it by saying he'd been smoking marijuana in her bed, licking her in the bathrooms of bars.

*My problem with Corinna was never her intelli-gence*, he'd said. *Have you seen her with those cross-word puzzles? It's just...you and I are going to col-lege...*

*Well, I'm mostly drinking.*

*Let's not even talk about what I'm doing.* He chuck-led self-deprecatingly. *This girl here...I just wonder what the appeal is for you.*

I thought about waking up at noon on a week-end, wet weather, slouching into the living room to find Corinna in her fraying camisole, mason jar full of sugary milky tea, reading some bad romance.

*When she sleeps on my chest*, I said, *she wraps her legs around my legs, falls asleep in a few seconds. It's beautiful. You must know from you and her how per-fect that feels.*

*I don't know,* he said, *I always felt like she had hygiene problems.*

*No.*

*She has a thing about showering.*

*But that's what you want. You want to smell...*

*I don't want to talk about Corinna's body with you anymore.*

I'd make tea for myself, too. I didn't usually like it, but I'd drink it with her. I'd sit next to her and leaf through poetry. Half an hour later, we'd curl on the couch again. I'd ask her if she remembered kissing me the night before, and she'd say no, she didn't.

*Wait a minute,* Bill said. *What's Paul doing while you guys are in bed?*

*Well, this is before Paul moved in with me. He doesn't get stoned anymore but funny the first thing we did was light up. Christened it.*

I could hear from the rush of air that Bill had stepped outside.

*I'm looking out over the beautiful vista of Long Island.*

*Anything good?*

*Nah.*

One or two cars honked. A bird or a door hinge sounded. Or a pair of brakes squealed.

*So, he just sort of ended up there in bed with you both?*

*Yeah, I guess he was the catalyst.*

*Or you were.*

I pictured tenement stairs from a film about

cheap artists, Bill mounting them.

*So tell me about this girl. What's she like?*

*Well, speaking of hygiene issues...*

*Nah,* I said, *you want that earthy, hands-in-the-peat smell.*

*Yeah, bog, musty cunt. No, just, I take care of myself. You know, if I have a problem, I address it. And I expect girls to be even better at it.*

*I haven't showered in three days.*

*Like, a girl's shower. There's nothing like a girl's shower. All the soaps...*

*To be honest, I've been a little depressed.*

I can hear the ocean. Bill said, *I want a boat.*

*I'm going to jump out of the window into the alley. You'll hear some poetry, then a splash.*

*Don't talk to me that way.* Bill started up a car. His. I was wrong about the stairs. *Clearly, you're in love with both of them. And you feel left out of the marriage. But it's a marriage, Jack. You have to respect that. The older I get...*

*I...*

*Admit it. You're in love with both of them and you wish things were just the way they were. You wish you all lived together. It doesn't work that way, though. People can't live that way. I know we used to talk about...we'd say it was all about all of us. But I think, you know, what are we?*

I looked around the place. The posters of movies Bill had originally recommended. The joke teacup that Corinna gave me. The joke is that it looks as though it's spilled, but the tea's spilled plastic. I glued it to the ceiling.

*Admit it. Are they there now?*

*No. They're on their way up.*

The teacup was a mistake, out of place on the careful paint.

*Did you ever…you don't have to answer me, but did you and Paul ever…*

*No.*

Bill's quiet. *I would just think that it would be hard, with all of you together.*

*No. Yeah, nah.*

# Winter

BILL HEFTED *THE RECOGNITIONS*.

"Did you read this?"

"Yeah, sure. I actually took a semester off. No, just open it at random."

"Ach*em*, 'The subway stopped under a river. It stayed there for minutes, while the occupants looked at one another, surreptitiously, appraising the company with whom they were trapped to meet disaster.' That's cool."

"Sounds like *The Waste Land*, right?"

Bill turned like a wind-up bird and began to hunt for it.

"Across from the window." I pointed. "Right… there."

"Listen to this," he said, having grabbed the *Collected*. "Early on in the book, 'I have measured out my life with coffee spoons.' Good, right? Now later, 'We are the stuffed men, headpieces filled with straw.' Ah! Now the end…here…" He read in the same portentous voice, "*The Rum-tum-tugger is a curious cat. If you offer him a rat, he'd rather have a mouse.*"

"*If you offer him a mouse*," I carried it.

"You memorized his *shit*?"

"Well…" I was sorry. "I saw *Cats* when I was a kid. Haven't you *seen* it? Isn't that what you *do* in New York?"

"Oh, ex*act*ly." He tilted his chin. "We spend the afternoon at the MOMA, drinking absinthe and cutting ourselves so we can feel something, then we smoke opium in a little, just a small den in China-town, talking about Céline, then we go see *Cats*."

I keep typing:

```
Subway stoped. Where to?
Allaboardalrightout out
An old man on a train.
A woman on a train with an
old man. Her father. They are
seated when the play begins.
Sound of a rush
```

Through the empty window in the wall I could hear Bill clinking in the kitchen.

"How about we start it on a train?" I shouted.

"Why?"

"Well…I dunno, let's throw ideas. We can have some text overhead, some train text like the Eliot poem, and some cut-ups. Then a rushing sound."

"You're thinking too far ahead." He crept into the room with his hands full, setting a whiskey with ice and two of the Adderall on the table.

"What's the reason we're starting on a train? What's this even about?" He stood staring out of the window at the gray mist and the staggered roof-tops, gardens with chimneys. His red hair looked dark in the diffused light.

"Well, I don't know if you can know what it's about until…let's start with a text, an ur-text, and work from there."

"An ur-text?"

"Right. We'll get a bunch of texts together and cut them up and make an ur-text. We'll start with Eliot…"

I fed a new sheet of paper into the typewriter and, when I looked up, Bill was shooing me out of the chair with his hands. "Comeonout."

Up, lightheaded, I drained my iced whiskey and looked in the mirror on the side of the big shelf. Bill displayed no evidence of whiskey but I already felt sly. The pill made me wonder if I'm always pale and exaggerated, and not just when I'm drunk.

"Where's your bible?"

I found it and paged through Leviticus. Looking up to the mirror, I tried to picture myself with his red hair.

"And the two kidneys, and the fat that is upon them."

"Slower."

"And the caul above the liver. It he shall take away."

Bill typed steadily. "See if you can find some, like, 'Thou shalt.' We want some of that. Give me the book." He opened a series of books on the table and looked quickly from one to the other, typing whatever his eyes fell on, I guess.

```
A heap of broken and the barn
fell

Our pains are answer to our
prayers

She plays his room again, alone
Where thou has ridden, there
must thou
```

"This is not subversive," Bill said. "This is just words. We need some kind of real experience, some raw…"

"We could take a walk out in the cold." I was flushed.

"In the Back Bay? Yeah, that's edgy."

"Let's take the car out somewhere…"

"Walden Pond?"

"No…" I said, "tourists, and we're pretty obviously high. How about we visit Corinna and Paul? Walk out on those breakwaters?"

Bill, pained, "You want to see *them*?"

"Well, we could just stay there. I mean down… we walk down to those breakwaters…"

"Yeah, I know. We used to go out there in high school…did you ever go there with Corinna?"

"No," I said, "but she and I and Paul keep talking about going down there with wine. I guess they used to set off fireworks there. Maybe when it's warm."

Bill lit on the typewriter. "Keep thinking about it."

```
Ben: I said it was like liquid
```

```
night, remember?

Angela: There's some potato
chips. Do you want some potato
chips?

Ben: I mean the first time we
came out here.

Angela: There's grease on your
fingers. Wash them in the ocean
before you touch me.

Ben: Well if you're worried
about getting your clothes
greasy…

Angela: You're a nasty boy.
That's what you are.

Ben: Take 'em off and let's go
in the water.

Angela: That water's cold. We'd
have to keep our clothes on.
```

Bill creaked back in the chair. "Where are those pills?"

"It looks like those are the last things you need."

"Oh, so you're a psychopharmacologist!" Bill got up and turned the corner into the kitchen. Through the little window, I could see him opening the bottle and popping two in his mouth.

"Bibliomancer. You mind if I take a turn?"

"You wanna gimme a chance?" Bill smacked the bottle down.

I'd have asked him to toss it my way, but since the yellow walls of the room were getting granulated and parting…

"Bill, I don't stand up and do something…"

"Go." He pointed his arm decisively. "Look for ur-text."

I walked to the right-most corner of the right-most bookcase. I opened the first collection I saw. *Out on the lawn I lie in bed*. Paul and Corinna's backyard garden.

"Yeah, let's go to Walden. Let's go right now, dude."

Bill looked up. He'd been working.

"It's snowing. It's just started."

"Fuckit let's go."

"Wait!" he said, rummaging in his backpack. "I've got some codeine in here."

"With the Adderall," I said, "that'll be perfect. Star's getting painkillers now!"

"What?" he looked up. "Star? When I think about Star I picture like, a little Corinna. But pixy-ish, tagging along."

"Yeah, she was always like, *What's going on, guys?*"

Bill made eyes like an eager puppy, looked up.

Since we were leaving, I picked up my spurs and slipped the leather strap over the toes of my boots up to where they rested against the heels. I buckled them in place. "She wants to be bad. She's hanging out with this girl, Mara. Corinna's way jealous."

"I'm sure," Bill said, brushing dust from the floor off his coat.

In the car, on the way, I started to notice how my fingertips were numb, even with the heat blasting.

"Did Burroughs write something about driving stoned?"

"Yes."

I tried to find it in my head, hold it, make it real. It would be a street sign to the Walden I wanted in with.

# Walden With Us

BILL LOCATED OLD RAILROAD TRACKS. THEY MAY have been past use, grass growing over the rails.

"I'm gonna walk down there," he said. "Have you got a cigarette?"

On the long drive down, getting lost and finding our way, my concentration had swung from oblivion to daze. Now, the drugs and the flask of Bushmills were working with me. *I see what I do. I am haloed.*

"Bill." My throat felt good. "Walk back a little ways. Farther. Good. Now come toward me."

I clicked the shutter and waited for the hum as he slouched down the center of the tracks, cigarette dangling.

"You look like a Beat."

We'd gotten lost on the way there, more high than drunk. Leaving Boston, Bill had lit one of the joints he'd rolled at the apartment. "Only…" he blew dramatically, "if you promise it won't distract your driving."

"There's Norwegian studies, it actually makes you better."

The codeine was driving. We entered a rosary of

rotaries. I fumbled in the armrest for the camera.

"Smile."

Bill pinched his face, glowered expressionist.

"So should I read from Emerson?" he asked, pulling out the book of essays I'd grabbed at the last minute.

"*An innavigable sea washes with silent waves between us and the things* blah blah. *Grief, too, will make us idealists.*"

He nodded. "'Grief will make us idealists.' Are *we* idealists?"

"Absolutely."

"I'm not so sure." He looked out of the window at the gray line of shops that hitch Boston to its suburbs: Staples, The Ground Round.

"Sure we are," I said where the road split three ways.

"Yeah. Of course we are." He sat back hard and turned his head.

The sky had the pale wash of drugs wearing thin.

"We're writing a grand play in verse," I said, "that will assure us fame."

"Verse plays are dead."

I turned onto a shaded exit. We were out of the city. I thought about the few things we'd been able to type back at the apartment. I tried to concentrate, but they were slippery.

"We've got a girl and her father on a train," I said, "we've got that."

"*Why* are they there?"

"Well, maybe he's taking her to college. They're

riding the train together so he can situate her."

"What's the tension? You need tension."

Bill pulled the bottle of pills out of his pocket and broke one in half. He swallowed one, told me to open up, and fingered half of it into my mouth.

"Body of Christ."

"Maybe," I swallowed, "he wasn't a good father. He abused her."

Bill was fast: "Too easy. How many abuse stories have you read?"

"Alright then." I slid in *Frank's Wild Years* and took another pull of the joint. I asked Bill to light me a cigarette and he said, "Can't you light one yourself? *Watch* it!"

I brought my foot down on the brake just in time to keep from hitting a thin woman in a huge leather buckle-laden jacket in the middle of traffic. She stood in front of the car for a long second, stared at us.

"What the fuck are you doing, dude? Go around her!"

At Walden, I marched down the old tracks while Bill framed a shot.

"Got it."

"It's too bad that girl from the road isn't here," I said and smiled. "We could take turns frightening her. You know, I could wait until she wasn't looking and holler."

Bill said, "We should have given her a drink." I unscrewed the flask.

"Yeah," I said. "Ma'am, I'm clearly under the influence of several drugs. You are either with us or against us."

"Who are you," Bill jabbed his finger at her shade and laughed, "to *ruin* our good time?"

"She was on her way to get some drugs," I said knowingly. "Look at her, spent, *ol' junkie smell with the liquid fingertips, straining in the junk sick dawn.*"

"*Black Ass Sally?*"

"My grandfather used to cash his checks at Black Ass Sally's in the thirties. I think she was white."

"*That furtive look. The tingle of junk sickness, hunger for the sweet meat.*"

"I can't believe we're the only ones here." Bill's breath looked like smoke. The snow had only been falling lightly and even seemed to be stopping. The beautiful combination of drugs we'd swallowed enabled me to feel the snow without the cold. The icy water leaking into my boots through the lace-holes felt good. My shell shivered without me.

"He's been trying to tell her some secret," I said. "He's telling her why he's been a bad father. He knows she's going to school way across the country and he knows why." I inhaled the air deep. It was cold and white. A few blackbirds wandered across the clear ovals of ice on the pond. I wondered how the ice could be oval like that.

"What's the incident?" Bill asked. "An incident to begin the action."

"Um." I scanned the frost, the heavy trees. "The train hit a car."

"Why?"

"Well we can gather all the people in the car. It'll be about them too. I mean we can tie time in too, like a thriller. They're so absorbed in the crash and he…he leaves without telling her anything. Then he dies. So he can't tell her…"

"It's hard to dramatize nothing. Where are you coming from? There's questions in…what are you trying to say?"

"I'm…Bill." I started laughing. "I've got nothing to say. I'm a blank slate. There's…I know you think you've had a loyal friend, someone who understands you, *symp*athizes." I grabbed my chest, fingers dramatic. "But there's nobody home! I'm…"

I could feel the cold then as I turned my head, wet hair in my eyes. I felt floored by how empty the landscape was except for us. There was only white around the pond.

"I can't imagine living here for a year," Bill said, stiffening. "What the hell did he do?"

"Maybe Emerson came by and they played Russian roulette."

Bill laughed, mimed a drunken click, bang.

"Does this end? This isn't Walden river, right?"

"I don't know. I've only read about it."

Walking in the cold air made my throat feel good again. I could trace the red vessels in my palms and fingertips.

"We'll just keep walking, be discovered ten years from now."

"Eating red berries for sustenance."

The sky glowered dark white.

"I'm going to see how far I can walk out onto that ice," I said.

"I don't want to have to call your parents."

"Shut up. Get out the camera."

# Smack

"Look at that." Paul pointed to the water where a couple of jellyfish drifted by the boardwalk.

"They travel in pods?"

"My wife told me they're called *smacks*."

"Like a murder of crows."

"Right." He grinned his perfect teeth. "Hard to murder someone with a jellyfish."

"Not pointy enough."

"So…" He squared his shoulders like he did before a little theater, mimed a man delicately picking a jellyfish out of the water, turning it over in his hand, smacking me with it.

I heard the hum of Corinna's boat motoring up to the dock as Paul set his Panama straight and a few tourists or awkward locals strolled by. She'd landed a job at the start of the summer — she was piloting a boat, taking small groups out to the edge of the inlet, along the coast of a few towns, and back in just over an hour. Corinna's tour was one of four or five businesses her uncle owned, and was centered entirely around a refurbished 1930s cabin cruiser called *Ticonderoga*.

"I don't really know how to pilot a boat that big,"

Corinna said, right after he offered her the job.

"You can do anything," I said, although I didn't believe it.

But she clearly could or else she'd have been terrified as she slowed and killed the motor just in time to sidle up to the dock. I jumped ahead of Paul to catch the line she waved. I managed to grab it in one try and lash it quick and tight to the cleat. The motor putted twice. A middle-aged, Manitoba-sized woman was first ashore when Corinna launched into her wrap-up talk. Paul took Manitoba's hand.

"Thank you, young man!" she said, emphasizing each word more than the last.

Paul tipped his hat.

"Paul!" Corinna shouted from onboard, and he hopped up onto the deck. He'd help her unload, they'd talk. Feeling alone, I wandered over to the wooden bench by the drifting jellyfish and took in the famous pizza shop, the carpet showroom on the hill pulling in cars like yo-yos, the cautious traffic over the drawbridge.

Paul and I had visited the bookstore that morning after a breakfast of cold cuts and rank cheese. I'd spent my time scanning the poetry section for something other than the wives of famous heroes, Mother's Day cards. Charles Jodoin, Paul's new friend, stood out as proudly as he could in beige and raised white lettering. I bought his book, already feeling I was nearer a mystery.

I sat on the wood bench along the dock and

leafed through it, reading a few lines from the longer poems. There was always a word that held me up, *cicatrix* or *epigone*, or even something easy like *evanescent* that I thought I knew but couldn't put my hand on. There'd be a reference to an old war, or *the cold standard Breton Woods concealed.* But I knew it was real:

> Turn back the shade! Rend low
> The lying walls that hedge your lawn
> To see! See what? The sleepers manifold,
> Unhemmed by domesticity? Unfurl
> Our cloistered lives along an open field?

"Jack!" Corinna hollered. "Get off your ass and help us with the coolers!"

I hopped up, saving the page with my finger, and stepped unsteadily onto the boat. Corinna and Paul were making a pile of the beer and juice left in the coolers and dumping the ice overboard. Paul grinned and snapped a silver can.

"Give me two dollars for that Paul."

"Jack'll split it with me." He looked at me semi-imploringly, semi-smooth. I shook my head.

"Fine!" she sighed, "I'll pay for it. But this is the last one. Holy shit will you look at the water!"

For a beat, I thought someone had dropped pink dye in the sound. Then I realized it was jellyfish the sound was choked with. There was more pink than black in the water.

"What are they—migrating?" Corinna asked.

"I don't think they migrate," Paul said.

I looked up at the sky's pale blue. I realized how strange the world was for a second, then I forgot about it.

"I hope we didn't hurt them with the boat," Corinna said.

Paul laughed. I said, "Don't you know, they come back together if they're sheared apart. Schulup."

Corinna grinned. "Schulup."

She said she didn't have time to go out for lunch, she had to eat on the boat and then clean the boat. Paul and I were on our own.

"They only have one opening, orifice, for eating, shitting, fucking. Oh, wait, that's Mara I'm thinking about. Sorry. I don't know who the girls are. I think you can tell by the shapes under them, the four circles, how big they are. They're all water. Ten percent jellyfish, or maybe less. These are probably all going out to sea. They have to get out there quick because they don't live very long."

Corinna lectured on, but I liked it. Paul sipped his beer. I borrowed a sip.

"Do you think jellyfish are edible?" I asked him.

"Sure," he said, "Corinna and I went out for some the other night. We ate a bunch of stuff, jellyfish, eel."

"She actually ate that stuff?"

"She'll eat anything if I eat it first."

She and I stayed on deck while he went below for the head. She'd coiled some ropes on the foredeck and now she was stashing them in the hatches.

"My fucking mother," she started saying to the

ropes, finished saying to me, "is going to start showing the house. I guess she found a realtor."

"Are you and Paul included?" She ignored me, went back to stuffing.

"Paul…both of us want to find a place in Boston. Near you. Wouldn't that be great, living down the hall?"

"Do it. Do it. And Star's in town, too."

Corinna turned, stood looking at me. She had remarkable posture, prepped to move. I could never make the clothes on her body real. She was naked, she just didn't know it.

Paul came above deck and told me it was time for lunch.

"You boys go. Go and get drunk or something."

"Oh," Paul opened his eyes wide. "We'll get drunk!"

But we didn't. After lunch, Paul and I crossed Main Street and kept walking. We stopped at the Fourier Gallery for long enough to get the gist of a show about religious sculpture: colorless Greek reproductions with crayon limbs, Venus's broken arms replaced by Shiva's dozen. Apollo's torso wore a fire mask. I liked the Sri Lankan girls on the broken relief best, the way they cupped their breasts spilling over.

We were on our way to the town green, where I promised him I'd show him some of the stretches we'd practiced in my performance-poetry seminar. He chain-smoked, saying he was thoughtful. He was a world away from how at ease he'd seemed on the boat. But I think he liked to play cocky in front of Corinna. And so he won her. That, and he never asked her who he was.

"I feel like they missed the point," I said. "It was like, trying to say that inherited Greek culture is oppressive, or we should all be inclusive, but all those mythologies are equally sort of, uh, vibrant. I mean, the Greeks are better, really, than uh…"

"Sure."

"Paul?"

"Yeah."

"What's up?"

He paused there in the middle of the down drawbridge, and lit another cigarette off the butt. I couldn't tell which of his gestures were theater and which so often rehearsed they'd become second-nature.

"Nah," he said, shaking his head, snarling into a smile. "We're gentlemen of leisure today."

"For a change. I mean, you're a gentleman of leisure today, instead of, you know, sitting in your easy chair, in your library, with your beautiful wife in the pool, and your gin in your hand."

He shook his head.

"With your larder full of cheese and tea, car fully stocked."

He laughed for real. I guessed he probably still had that bottle of Sapphire tucked in the Plymouth's armrest.

I looked off the seaward side. "Look," I said. "There's Corinna's boat." It was no bigger than the white of my fingernail.

"She doesn't want to live here anymore," he said.

"Oh?"

"Yeah." He flicked the butt to sea. "Boston. Maybe Hawaii. From her romance novels."

"Does the cruise run out that far?"

A group of old women in pinned hair and neck brooches came toward us from the far end of the bridge. There was a priest with them, or a minister, I wasn't sure of the difference in costume. He had one of those white collars that wasn't notched but showed itself all around.

"Hey," I said, tapping Paul's shoulder, "remember what we used to do for those guys?"

Paul smiled and grabbed me by the shirtfront and stuck his tongue in my mouth, rolling it around. I ran my hand back and forth over his hair like an ape. We were both, I think, watching them out of the sides of our eyes. We got the tsk-tsk we wanted, bald heads turned, hurrying past.

I threw my arm around him in the breezy summer afternoon and we walked past the old men, past the lamp shop. Some waist-high girls were giggling by the monument.

"Jack," he said, "I'm a married man."

"Right," I said, pulling my arm away, "where's the sanctity?"

He clucked and shook his head.

"Corinna's restless."

Once we'd reached the center of the green, I took off my coat and tossed it by the cannon's bolted wheels.

"We're thinking about maybe finding a place near you."

I looked down at my shoes, let my head roll back and forth.

"Look down and just let it roll," I said. "First put your cigarette out."

He nodded and patiently drew a few more puffs before he rubbed the head off with his fingers and tossed his stub in the grass. Then he took off his linen sport coat, folded it neatly over the cannon's barrel, rolled up his sleeves.

"Let your head go loose. Roll it back and forth but not all the way around. Never all the way. Now roll your shoulders loose, relax a little…"

After we'd risen up again out of a ball-crouch on the ground and stretched our arms wide I looked around at the old women walking out of their white houses in the sunshine.

"Are you going to run for mayor?"

"What?"

"Let's go read," I said, and we found a spot in the shade of a willow where the grass was still thick enough to sit on. Paul smoked and read his Japanese etiquette book. *Never pass something to another with your chopsticks; this resembles the way in which some Buddhists pass the bones of the dead.* I read a few lines of Charles Jodoin and looked up and around, read and looked, never finishing a whole poem.

"Does Corinna seem happy?"

I felt the way I usually did pressed to understand

someone else's feelings, hopeless.

"She's twenty and she lives at her mother's house. I don't know. I think she's found you and she loves you. I think she's waiting for your life to begin."

He nodded. "She's lazy," he said and smiled, realizing he was being too hard on her. "Well, she has to finish school."

"What about you? Ever think about trying again?"

"I drive up to a house," he said, closing the book, "and put out my cigarette, check my teeth in the mirror, you know how I do, and by the time I get to the front door and knock on it, I'm there only for them, I'm whoever they want me to be."

I can feel my attention flagging so I concentrate on his excellent teeth.

"It's deeper than acting. No offense. I really do want to make them happy, to say what they want to hear. I want to reach into my pocket and pull out a contract. I want to sell."

"You've come pretty close to some sales, too, haven't you?" I treaded cautiously and it worked, he nodded deep.

"Very close."

# The Straw Bed

CORINNA SAID THE DOUBLE BED WHERE SHE SENT
me to nap used to belong to her Dad and his first
wife, the one who killed herself before he met her
mother. They bought the frame and mattress somewhere in Central Europe in the late fifties, just after the Bulgarian ceremony, traveling as part of a
cultural exchange program. The thing about the
frame, she said, is that it was designed to hold a
huge mattress filled with "tempered straw." Her
Dad told her a story about how it reminded them
of when they had to sleep in a hay loft once. But
the original mattress was long gone and had been
replaced by a queen-size American mattress too
narrow and too short for the frame.

I was daydreaming half asleep when she came
into the room, quietly stripped down to her under-
wear and crawled under the covers.

"Hey."

"Weren't you sleeping?"

I couldn't tell if I was tired or pretending to be
tired as I turned my head on the pillow. There were
a few car sounds from the street. Surprisingly, con-
sidering how close it was to Corinna's house, I was

never able to smell or hear the ocean.

"I'm tired too," she said, putting her arm around my chest, wrapping her bare leg around my blue jeans underneath the sheets.

Since she'd married Paul, this was the closest we'd been alone. I felt split between how comfortable I was—how comfortable I wanted her to be—and the movement of her bare leg.

And while we're being ridiculous, lying here like aspiring saints, what the fuck is marriage anyway but an ornamental restraining order? Who was I, who lived for her more than my father lived for America, with his flag-embroidered throw pillows, more than Charles Jodoin lived for poetry with his long beige books—who was I to be patient?

I couldn't be still but I didn't move much. We shifted against one another for the next half hour. I wound my fingers in the base of her hair. She brushed her face against my chest. I moved my thigh tight between her legs.

"You asleep?"

"No. You?"

With her head on my chest, there was no graceful way to kiss her. I was still unsure.

"Jack?"

"You?"

"Tell me a story. Tell me about *Maybe*."

We'd both had the same children's book. It was one of the things we talked about when we first got to know each other.

"There once was a Maybe from Maywhich," I recited, "who lived with a bird in his hair."

"What about the may witches? The women?"

"You're getting ahead of me."

"Sorry."

"And none of the maidens of Maywhich knew why, or knew how, or could care."

I unhooked her bra from the back and touched her breast.

I felt her breath warm through my shirt.

As I kept repeating the children's book, slowly, not sure what I was saying, I felt her cool fingers inside my shirt, moving up my belly and onto my chest. She fell back from me, left her face on my neck. Her breath came unevenly. Her hand warmed under my shirt.

"If you listened at night you could hear them… moving far from the lights of the town…"

I spoke into her hair. Her hair muffled it. With my free hand I tilted her chin up and kissed her. Only after a minute did she open her mouth, and then only a little. I kissed her and ran my hand along the side of her body where I felt her hesitate.

"Come here."

"I can't."

"What?"

"Paul."

"Fuck him," I said, and pulled her hair away from her face. I had no idea what was behind her eyes as she looked down at me. I realized then that I hadn't taken the spurs off my boots yet, that I was lying in bed with spurs.

"Jack, I can't."

"Fuck this." I rolled off the bed, found my cowboy hat and put it on. It was ridiculous, but I wanted to cover myself, indignant.

"What *is* this?"

"What?"

"You coming into bed. Taking your clothes off?"

"You're my best friend!"

"Your…is this how you act with Star? Fucking Star is your best friend! Are you kissing her? Marrying her friend what's-her-name?"

She lay on her back and looked at the ceiling, not moving.

"Why don't you come and sleep?" she said.

I took my shirt and spurs off and lay down next to her. She stayed on her side of the bed.

"This is obvious crap," I said. She was quiet, breathing steady. "You guys sign a fucking piece of paper and all of a sudden…I kissed Paul today, there was no scandal. I don't know why you don't do what you want to do. Unless you don't want to. Maybe you don't. But I want you to. I think you would if you…"

A quiet settled down on us, and after ten or fifteen minutes she started snoring a little. Her small nose, pinched at the bridge, made her snoring a usual sound. I thought of scattered nights in The Apartment, waking up with the sun coming in.

I sat up on my elbow and watched her sleeping, her mouth slightly open, the back of her bra still unfastened, one breast bare, her nipple pressed up on the wire. I guess she wasn't bothered.

I rose up, took my shoes and socks off, and walked downstairs quietly so as not to wake her. I would leave the spurs there that night. It was a deliberate habit I'd picked up early in high school. Still a freshman, I'd overheard a conversation between a senior couple, the girl saying, "You have so much stuff at my house, I don't even know what's mine anymore."

In the library, I sprawled myself in Paul's chair and picked up one of Corinna's novels.

> She dug up blades, bones, loose coins and dust. I was a nerve, peeled to its most attentive threads.
> "Have you made discoveries?"
> "Some. Small."

I liked it but I threw it on the table, looked down at my belly. I tried to pinch flesh and failed. I could have grabbed a handful six months earlier.

I heard the door open and shut. Corinna's mother was in the house.

"Hello, Jack."

In the years I'd known her I don't think she once looked me in the eye.

"Hi Bridget." Star and Paul called her *Mom*, but it felt affected.

"Are the kids here?"

"Corinna's asleep upstairs. Paul's out on the job."

"Well…" she said, putting her bags on the sofa, brushing her long gray hair, disappearing into the kitchen, "as long as he keeps working hard…"

Back in Boston, Corinna had confessed that when we were all kids and came home smelling like pot smoke and wine, I would always get the blame. Jack smoked, Jack drank. "Well, you left early and Bill and Star stayed over, so we had to make someone the bad guy." I didn't mind. I always assumed their parents would understand, especially Corinna's mom, with her long gray hair, wide eyes.

"What did you kids do today?"

"Well, Paul's been working. Corinna and I just sat by the pool."

"So…" she said, and we both let it hang there.

"I'm sorry," I said in bad faith, "sitting around…"

"Oh!" She waved in a gesture that had become a nervous second nature, coming back into the study, breaking my fantasy about owning it, pulling a few packages of tea from her knit bag.

"I hear they're thinking about Boston," I said.

"Well, Corinna's got to finish school. Then they can move where they want. I tell them, you know, whatever makes them happy."

She busied herself in the kitchen for a few minutes. I thought about making my way up for my shirt.

"Are you coming down at the end of the month?" she shouted.

"Yeah," I said, cocky, so I was asking for it, "I guess you've noticed we kinda alternate weekends."

"I'm surprised you're not coming down for the party at the end of the month."

"Huh?"

"Oh, I'm sure Paul told you about it. Charlie's party."

"Charlie?"

"Oh," she waved her hand, "I don't know him well. I mean Charles from next door."

"Charles Jodoin the poet?"

"They told you about it, right? Maybe it slipped... Paul's mind. I know he was excited about it."

"Did you ever meet him?" I asked, changing subjects.

"Me? Well. I met him a few times when Dom was alive. I think he was at the house once or twice. But I've been...you know I'm so busy, I don't keep up. He's only really here in the summer."

## Rebels at Walden

THOREAU WAS TEN FEET TALL FROM THE BASE OF the pedestal and wore a Roman toga. Folds of it draped on his arm. The bottom half of the statue was mossy. The inscription was in Latin anyway, so I didn't bother taking the letters in.

"Is this from when he conquered Gaul?" I asked.

"Yeah, you know, this is New England, Henry." Bill pointed at the bare stone shoulders. "You a little cold there?"

"Gladiator suit at the cleaners?"

Bill panted a laugh, "I don't think they had dry-cleaning."

"You're misinformed," I said. "There was a large Chinese transcendental community in Concord back then. That's where they got Zen from."

The snowfall calmed and the air warmed. I'd put my gloves in my pocket and I had been carrying my jacket over my shoulder ever since I handed Bill the backpack.

Bill pushed forward past the statue, stood up on a flat stone. He looked around.

"This seem like a good place?"

"Yes."

Bill pulled the little Underwood out of his knapsack and positioned it on the rock.

I unscrewed my flask and set it down.

"I thought we'd need this," he said, pulling one of my tin ashtrays out of his front pocket.

I cracked my knuckles like I'd seen on TV and fed in the page where we'd left off.

```
Zero: Your mother turned my
skull into a bowl.

Jackie: Are you saying she was…
what? a drunk?
```

I ran my fingers back and forth over the keys a few times. Tree rustle. No view of the pond from there, but a little creek past the rock. Bill paced by it.

```
Zero: You've always been
accusing me of something. What
is it actually that you accuse
me of?

Jackie. Nothing, Zero.
```

The edge of Bill's jaw over my shoulder means he's been reading while I type.

"Can I direct you somewhere?" I asked him.

"I thought…I don't know what you're doing but I thought he didn't touch her. When she was a kid, I mean. That's what we decided on."

"Yeah," I said, "I'm just gonna suggest it. Sort of let the audience wonder. Nothing serious. Then they talk about it and decide that the glances she always got from him weren't sex but love. Unsexual love."

"If she spurned him," Bill said, lighting a cigarette, "and that made him *more* interested…that's what happens."

"Doesn't have to be," I said. "If a dog doesn't pay attention to you, you may try harder, offer it food…"

"Let's talk about people, though. And I ignore those dogs."

I watched the back of Thoreau's toga ripple. Stone auspices.

"It wasn't ever sexual." I collected my thoughts. "She didn't want him to be her father and maybe she displaced or something those thoughts inside her that made it seem like…"

"Look!" Bill said, pointing at the page. "In your head, there's sexual tension there. The whole *zero/Zero* thing, which incidentally I don't like but never mind. They're flirting, Jack. You can't play with that if you're not going to use it. Remember Chekhov and the shotgun?"

"Fuck those rules. Who made that rule?"

"Chekhov."

"Who said that things had to have a certain structure? How about new forms? Plays with guns over the mantelpiece and they never go off. Storms where no one learns anything. Poems that don't begin."

"People already did all that. The modernists and everything. No one stayed in the theater. People left."

"They stayed," I said. "I'd stay."

Bill saw how ludicrous I was talking and spread his arms, reared his head back like he was going to let go a gut-howl. I waited as he sucked in air, but all that came out was a strangled bird-in-the-machine.

I mimicked it, blew one back at him even more unsplendorous. I threw my shoulders way back, posed my legs like Hamlet, opened my palms like a magician.

"Whrr! Rar-owl!"

Our throats hurt.

I climbed up on the statue of Thoreau, put my arm around his shoulders to haul myself up on the plinth.

"Take a picture. Come on, take a picture. Don't smoke. Come on, there's like twenty pictures left on the roll and I paid for them. Come on. In the junk…you can…no, look over there, in the junk sick dawn there's a fuckoff. Where you gonna go? In the woods? Take my fucking picture. Yeah. Yeah, it's good shit, read it. Yeah, *junk sick dawn*. I'm disarmed, perched I'm in our hero's arms."

"Look heroic like him," Bill said, "drape your coat on your arm."

# Under the Small Lights

"I don't know. I wouldn't want to be married to Corinna."

"What do you mean?" I asked.

"That girl is loose, man." Star had been bolder lately. We assumed it was because she'd been hanging out with Mara.

"Why? Do you mean in the past? She's a respectably married woman now. Aren't you in the sewing circle?"

Star didn't say anything, just poked at the car's tape deck.

"What's this? They sound in pain."

"Buddhist monks," I said. "The OM calls the universe to order…"

"I can't listen to this and talk at the same time. What else do you have?"

I told her what else I had.

"OK," she said. "But we're going to drink, not to Corinna and Paul's funeral, so let's listen to something good. Get in the mood."

The truth was I worried about getting in the mood. I didn't like to feel as though I could lose myself. There were people who could let go of themselves, people like Mara, the way Star had described her, and I wasn't one of them. I paid attention to how I lit each cigarette.

"So," I said, lighting one, putting the lighter in my pocket. "What have you heard about Corinna?"

"Jack," she said, "you're not still trying to get in her pants."

"No."

"Because you shouldn't."

"Right."

"Because they're married."

I'd taken the long drive there from home, but Star didn't mind because the chanting was replaced with early Cure and the ocean appeared. We would pass a row of houses, over a bridge, then we'd be at the bar.

Star was living with her parents over summer break. We both came from the same town about an hour's drive inland. Whenever I told people which one, they mistook it for a richer town on the opposite end of the state. We grew up listening to stories about how our city'd once been a whaling capital, then an exclusive summer resort, with working streetcars to take you as far as Mystic, a hardworking mill town, bastion for our square-faced, coarse-clothed progenitors. Now they were building a casino. In the meantime, our time, there was a lot of empty brick downtown, overgrown fields less than a mile out.

"You know what I don't get from Corinna, that I get from you," I said, "is that connection. That feeling that you're listening completely to what I'm saying, that I'm hearing you, that we're really connecting."

"Well," Star said, "yeah, that's why we're friends."

"Right, but I don't get that from Corinna."

I pulled the car into the unmarked lot behind Ricky Bang-Bang's. We could hear music through the back wall, a dry thump and a wind-up.

"I don't think you don't get it," Star said. "I just think it's not the reaction you want."

Paul was already standing outside by the time we turned the corner, sucking a cigarette, chatting with an older guy with worn-looking skin and close-cropped dark hair. He nodded hello as we approached but his mouth kept moving. I lit a cigarette and stood myself beside him while Star went inside to look for Corinna.

"We have to, with the advance from *Walls* so low."

"And you're their showboat."

The guy rolled his eyes. "Charlie doesn't care. He hasn't renegotiated…"

I looked between two of the bigger townhouses where you could see notches of the ocean. Through the dark I thought I could make out a white bird perched on one of the pylons. No, it was a boat, small because it was far off, doubtlessly racing where it seemed to be inching.

"I'm gonna head in."

Paul nodded and I walked through the door, past the dusty anchor in the small hallway, the ol' captain statuettes and black & white pictures of past proprietors and into a large oak-and-faded-brass room and "You're So Pretty." The crowd Paul called *the summer people* were still here, although they wouldn't be for long. The summer people were renters and didn't buy lawnmowers. You could tell them from the locals because they were always having fun or trying to look like it. The locals were quiet, beautiful but faded, like Paul's friend outside. My eye caught a pink shirt, starched, on the back of what I figured was a summer person, drinking martinis with his tan wife. She wore jeans rolled up and touched his drink hand when she laughed.

Corinna pressed next to me. "Summer people?" I asked, running my hand down her bare arm. I sniffed her head. I liked the way her shampoo smelled, even a few days after she'd washed. Now, for example. The stronger she smelled the better I liked it.

"You sound like Paul. No that's Tad and Martha. Tad used to run the boat out."

"Ah! I'm *bad* at this."

"Yeah, sweetie, you kinda are. Like, look at that guy over there in the jacket. No, the blue one."

"Ah!"

"Summer person. Is Paul hobnobbing?"

"Yeah, I think he'll be running for office here."

She stepped back and narrowed her eyes. Star does it the same way now from watching Corinna. "Yeah, you know I've lived here my entire life and he already knows more people than I do."

"Well he's sold them all lawnmowers."

"And that's another thing. He and I have to have a talk about that."

"Lawnmowers? He'll be game. It's kind of his pet subject, now. You know he's got *me* talking about…"

She shook her head. I saw that she was holding a nearly empty Corona by her hip. If it had been full she'd be spilling it. "No, not lawnmowers. Yes, lawnmowers—he hasn't…I shouldn't tell you this."

"You should tell me everything. I'm like a doctor."

Paul came in the door and looked around the room. I saw him watching Star step out of the bathroom. Then he found us and pushed through the crowd.

"I think I'm kidding myself about everything," I said. "I'm kidding myself about everything in my life."

"Yeah," she said smiling, tossing it off. "Well you're not the only one, honey." She looked steady at me for a second. The conversation had gone the only place I could take it.

"Go talk to Star," she told me.

Corinna stiffened when I squeezed her arm. I started pushing across the room. Star saw me coming and began walking toward me. Instantly, the room was more crowded than when I'd come in. Bars reach a tipping point. I felt a little jolt when I touched Star's shoulder. I'd never felt a jolt from her before.

"Let me get you a drink."

"Rum and Coke. Wait. That's not what I like. What is it that I like?"

"You like vodka and Coke."

"No I don't, that sounds disgusting."

"You liked it the other night. Remember, you were surprised by how okay it tastes?"

She stepped back and narrowed her eyes. "Is that what you and Bill drink when you have your drunken weekends?"

"Yes." I held her eyes, felt them stammer shy. *See how easy this is*, I thought on the way to the bar. *You can do this all the time. Fuck Corinna, stop thinking about her. You can make her into someone new in your head, turn the lens, fix her.* But I couldn't tell the inside of my head to lie. I bought a couple of straight Cokes and turned my back on the bar to tip them over with a little vodka from my flask. I stirred them, sucked my finger and moved halfway between Star and Corinna. I curled the same finger for Star to follow.

"We're the last confederacy of good people on earth," I said when we were all together, but the music was too loud for the girls to hear me over their talk, or for Paul to hear over his attention to the room.

It was Bowie, and for a long time after that I still thought he was singing, *smoke me like the rain.*

Seeing no one was listening I offered, "I'm lazy and never want to do good work. You know…you know why people pay attention to David Bowie and not Charles Jodoin, or me for that matter, is that there's documentary evidence that David Bowie left his house…"

Halfway into the word *Bowie* Paul turned to me and smiled like he knew my rhythm meant I'd hit a point he could assent to. Paul could sniff out a truism in a room full of exhaust. "Star!" I said, pinching my fingers, touching my lips. It would have been one hundred times more subtle if I'd shouted, "Do you want to smoke some pot?"

She nodded her head, and we moved back through the crowd past the pool table crowd and dart-board crowd and the let's-hang-out-by-the-screen-door crowd and out the back screen door into a whiff of the alley's sweet summer trash.

"Do you want to go into your car?"

"No, how about just two blocks past that alley then right, then left, and then the ocean's right there."

She looked at me skeptically. I produced the joint from the Zodiak box I'd searched all of Boston to find and lit the little pinched end.

"I've got…" she started and stopped herself. "Never mind."

"Okay."

I could see both ends of the alley from where we stood, should someone walk down either I'd have plenty of time to snuff the little thing.

"I've got … a little something from Mara for later."

"Okay."

She looked up, blushing in the dark.

"I thought about not telling you and keeping it all for myself." She smiled a little, proud of that.

"Well, break it out now."

"No," she said, taking a deep drag in, then two little ones, filling her lungs, breathing out. "They're for later."

Inside, Paul and Corinna were dancing. The band was surprisingly gentle. I always loved watching Corinna dance and, even though my feelings about her and Paul couldn't change, I had to admire the way they moved together. She had the small problem of the professional dancer who can't turn off the performance, but she moved like a well-rehearsed dream. For once, Paul wasn't distracted.

I glanced at Star next to me, her dark hair dyed burgundy, her freckled skin, stub of a nose. I thought about how awkward we would look on the floor: me tall in black leather and her pocket-sized in khaki shorts.

"Come on," I said.

"Really?"

"Come on."

"Jack, I'm too stoned to dance."

So I left to buy and spike another Coke. When I got back the song had changed and the three of them were sitting at a table by the floor. No one else was dancing.

"Nothing for me?" Paul asked when I set the glasses down.

"You were busy with love."

"Seriously, though," Corinna said. "I don't want

to spend any more money."

"Well that's no trouble."

Paul cut me off with, "I was just talking Corinna into going down to the boat."

"Do you have anything to drink on the boat?"

"I don't want to drink anymore," Corinna said.

"Okay," I said, "but I have a friend named Corinna who would never say anything like that."

The band started playing something we all recognized but couldn't place. We sat there silently, squinting eyes at each other, opening our mouths like we were going to guess and then thinking better of it.

*See the marketplace in old Algiers...*

Corinna and Paul decided it was stupid for anyone other then Patsy Cline to sing "You Belong to Me." But the woman on stage pronounced the words softly and slow like a careful report.

Paul and Corinna were off dancing before I could say anything. Star leaned in to whisper but I couldn't understand. Her mouth too close in my ear. For someone who was starting to take drugs seriously, Star had one of the lowest drunk thresholds I knew.

"What?"

She shook her head, looked down at the brown film of drink at the bottom of her glass and finished it.

"Come on," I said, standing up and taking her hand. Corinna and Paul were dancing slower than the pace of the song demanded. His hands hovered low on her waist and she kept her lips close to his. I piloted Star under the small lights in front of the band. She moved hesitantly, like she didn't dance very often. I tried not to think about Paul and Corinna while Star and I shifted, holding each other's arms at first. Corinna's belly was all muscle, but Star's gave to the touch. I held her waist and moved my thumbs a little. But I looked up when I shouldn't have and saw Corinna and Paul pressed hard together. She pulled back, looked at him, and quickly licked the side of his face.

I don't know what made me think Star would be comfortable if I kissed her but I did. I touched her face at the temple, ran my finger down her cheek and lifted her chin. The way she kissed me back, expectantly, comfortably, it was as if she didn't know why I wanted to. I was careful not to watch Corinna from the corner of my eye.

We stepped onto the cabin cruiser *Ticonderoga* in the dark. Corinna disappeared into the cabin to find some flashlights and cigarettes. Star and I walked to the bow separately, not touching one another for fear of doing something too decisive. On the drive down we'd said little to each other, both unsure if the kiss had changed anything. I hoped it hadn't but, truth be told, I wasn't thinking about it, just watching Corinna in the rearview.

"Jack wants to be Leonard Cohen," Corinna said, listening to the music.

"Who do you want to be?" I asked her.

"I want to be Star," she said, smiling at Star who turned around and smiled back.

Now Paul was standing next to me and Star had disappeared into the cabin with Corinna.

"You should be paying more attention to your date," Paul said.

"Star? When did she become my date? Does that mean Corinna's yours?"

He said, "You'll have to ask her."

As he and I spoke, we gradually advanced ourselves to the edge of the bow, an unspoken test of bravado, until half of our shoes reached over the water.

"You've been trying to spit something out for a couple of weeks now."

Paul didn't like being challenged. He took off his panama and ran his hand through his thick hair, reset the hat.

"Why don't you go down and get them and the beer," he said, working to balance.

I met Star coming up from the cabin and we reached for each other awkwardly on the way past. We touched at the heels of one another's hands, let our fingers run the length of our arms until we separated. I lowered myself down the steps carefully, the way I was once told to do on boats and compulsively never lost touch of. There was a bare bulb glaring on the side of the cabin, but it was otherwise dark. I found Corinna with her hands around a few bottles of the tour's Red Stripe, staring at herself in the galley's mirror.

"We're old, Jack."

"We're twenty."

"Oooo," she winced, "don't say it." She shut her eyes and shook her head like make-the-bad-man-go.

"With our rotting teeth," I said.

"Yeah, and our wrinkly foreheads." She found our groove.

"Flaccid, crooked penises."

"Wrinkly, dusty cunts."

I leaned against the doorframe, my hands in my pockets. We shared a beat when our eyes caught, but I didn't move toward her and the moment passed.

"Go upstairs and see Star." She looked me in the eye.

I reached for the bottles of Red Stripe. I wanted to grab both of her hands and pull them toward me. I wanted to slap her face.

Star and Paul were talking about old times on the deck in the starlight.

"Paul was saying he wishes he went to high school with us."

Paul smiled. "I was saying I wish I knew Corinna back then."

"She was with Bill back then," I said, opening the Red Stripes against the brass rail, handing them out. Star reached out to take my hand after I eased myself down along the side of the cabin where they were sitting. I didn't know how close she wanted to get but I wanted to touch her. Her fingers were damp and cold. When she let go, I felt a large pill in the center of my palm.

I tried to catch her eye but she stared out blankly at the water. Much of the Star I knew was composed of parts of Corinna she'd caught or memorized. Still, I felt at a loss to watch her change into someone more like Mara. I recognized her low threshold for imitation. Seeing how Bill paused a little before answering any question in a way that centered the action on his answer, I'd started doing it myself. Recently, I'd noticed myself unconsciously copying the way Paul ran the tip of a cigarette around the inside rim of an ashtray, never tapping it. But to see Star taking on what I was convinced were Mara's tics (who else?) — the way she tossed her head to move the hair from her eyes, or wearing the same shirt three or four days in a row — made me feel unsteady. I put the pill in my mouth and swallowed it.

"I'm going to go back down," I said, "get some water."

"Get me some," Star said. I climbed below again and startled Corinna on the boat's satellite phone. She looked at me like an intruder. I held up a finger, poured myself a glass of water at the faucet and went back upstairs. When I told Paul she was on the phone he drifted to the cabin. Star and I were left alone, cross-legged, near enough our knees touched.

"What did you give me?"

"Vicodin."

"Thanks. Nothing hard?"

"Maybe later." She didn't mean tonight.

We heard raised voices from the cabin.

"They fight too much," she said as though she were making a point.

"You think?"

My mouth was nice and dry and things were moving slowly. I drank more beer.

"I was always surprised," I said, "that Corinna never went for me. I mean we have more of a…I mean, I think she's more comfortable with me than…"

I heard Paul's voice go high, but the distance drained the words apart.

"I mean listen to her," I went on, "she's obviously not happy. But…" I held Star's eyes. I wanted her present. "I'm happy here. I like this, that we can talk this way. How I don't feel guarded with you."

I looked to see if she were flustered, but I heard them clapping up the stairs and got distracted.

"Summer three years ago," I said, wresting myself back, launching, "I thought we were all this perfect intimacy, like we were part of a painting or a sculpture, whole like that."

Corinna and Paul were above deck now, lowering and positioning themselves beside us, but I wouldn't be deferential, I'd hold my world.

"Remember, Jack, you showed us the tape you made of all those softcore movies on Cinemax?" Corinna said. "Paul, when Jack was a kid he used to know where the sex scenes were in all these softcore movies."

Paul looked distracted.

"Yeah, well," I said, "I got home twenty minutes before my parents, so I guess I had a narrow window."

"Jack was so nervous when he showed us those tapes. But you were obviously, um, proud of them." Corinna laughed at Paul.

Star said, "Yeah, my dad used to tape those! He would tape something for me and they would be on the end of it! It would always be someplace hot like Florida or something."

"And you'd get that jazz music," I said to Star. "That solo sax brrrr brr-up-up."

"Yeah," Corinna said, "Jack didn't just tape them, he made like a mix tape." Corinna tried to cue my eyes. The Vicodin helped me let it go.

"But. I think they had all the ingredients I lacked. I mean, this is before I went to college or read anything, I mean, I'm twelve, so what do I know about art? But here there's naked people putting on masks and music that, you know if it wasn't 'erotic' it would be…" We started interrupting each other.

Star smirked. "So you figured that's what women were? These perfect, naked beings you could control?"

"No," I said, "I thought that's what life was. I mean, I thought there was some compartment of life I could access that would be just… And I liked it when they took place in that garbage truck light, when you all fell into my life, I mean, I would drive away from one of our houses at four a.m. and be worried about getting home before my parents woke up, but also amazed by… I was lifted without questioning it into a world where the pines were like palms. It was Rhode Island but it was tropical."

"I love how you talk about it," Star said. "Like reality should change just for you."

"I'm that important," I said, knowing I'd pushed myself past that conversation. They kept talking but I drifted, and everyone I looked at looked away.

# Crazy Horse

"YOU KNOW, AS A PERFORMANCE PIECE," I SAID, tapping away at the going-nowhere scene. "This, *this...*"

"Yeah," Bill said, "I think Thoreau was the first one..." He gestured toward the small, preserved cabin across the lake. I couldn't imagine it wasn't a re-creation. Even in New England.

"I probably should actually read Thoreau one of these days," he said.

"No rush," I told him. "Why not start with the Bible and work your way up?"

"I've never even read *Moby Dick*," Bill said. "Not really. I haven't read all those modern, cool authors but I love them. I fill my bed with their books."

"Totally," I said, "I roll around in them."

The late afternoon air didn't deepen so much as pale, turning dark blue only at the edge, where the tree-line deepened. Our collective high reached a loopy summit. We may already have been coming down.

"I got an encyclopedia," I said, "and I was flipping through it and I had to check twice, but Gertrude Stein was born only forty years after Mark Twain.

Only ten years after Edith Wharton. Eighteen-seventy something. She would have been middle-aged when our grandparents were kids, you know? She published all that experimental stuff before they were born. And they elected Reagan."

"American history's not that long," Bill said. "Put your hand in the ground, you'll get blood on your fingers."

I watched wind in the leaves move shadows and light on the page still stuck in the typewriter.

"It must be so nice to live around here," Bill said, "all that history preserved. All the buildings in Boston…" I looked up at the way the toga folded around the base of Thoreau's neck. If I concentrated for a second I could detect the muffled sound of traffic. We were near a road. The road was near the pond.

"You've got lots of history in New York."

Bill shook his head. "Some. But they don't…they don't care for it. Something historic is something in the way. They just tear things down."

I started typing. Just because it had been a while since one of us typed.

```
Jackie: Look at these fields.
They'll be covered one day.

ZerO: Wise. But all you see is
ashes.

Jacie: You own a smoke shop.

Zero: So what rew you saing .
```

```
Are you saying. ?

Jackie: that its all

Zero: It's a cold day. There's
a blue wind. There's nothing at
sea.
```

I stared at the typewriter. I couldn't make something happen. The page blurred when I read it.

"We should get back," I said. The cold that had settled in my hands for twenty minutes was reaching up my arms. I felt it blush in my spine.

"You want to finish a scene first? Or at least decide on a scene?"

"How about we don't invade North America, but instead the Indians invade us," Bill said. We were walking back toward my car. Time jumped at me furiously. "They gang up — let's say they crossed the land bridge a few hundred years earlier than they did, so they have time to organize — and they cross the Atlantic in canoes…all of them. And maybe they just attack England, because Europe would be too considerable."

"Wouldn't Europe rally to England's defense?" I stopped feeling the cold. Bill's talk distracted me out of it.

"Nah. They make a treaty with France. They're good at that. Frenchies figure anything that fucks up England is good for them."

"So what do they do, set up a little paradise there? Wipe out English?"

"It's just so much better than what happened,"

Bill said, looking at the pressed dirt and rocks patched with snow. He carried the typewriter. I was shaky.

"Really?"

"We should write about Crazy Horse. Do you know anything about him?"

"No."

Bill shuffled the backpack against his other shoulder. I felt my numb toes tingle in the walk. It was all my own fault for wearing cowboy boots all winter. That, and the slips on ice should have taught me. And the way the cheap showoff spurs got bent from the pedals when I drove.

"He went on a vision quest. His father was a shaman, but he did it alone. His vision told him to never keep anything for himself, to be beneficent. And never to let anyone hold his shoulders back. And to dress simply, just a stone behind his ear."

I was quiet for a minute. When he didn't say anything, I asked, "What did Crazy Horse do again? I don't think I ever knew."

"Custer. And he lived his whole life according to the vision. I wish I had that strength."

"*The vision at Walden.*"

"*The vision at Walden.* Spin your own clothes."

"Take amphetamines," I said. "Smoke, um, French cigarettes. How are we going to fit Crazy Horse in a play about a girl on a train? Or is that what it is now?"

"I don't like the train," Bill said loud. I pictured how different I would be if I lived generously, dressed simply.

"Train stuff doesn't work. Outdated. What about her already having arrived? Her father's gone. Her new life begins?"

"I don't know a Mohawk from an Iroquois."

"That's our fault," Bill said, setting the backpack down to roll his shoulders. He didn't say any more but the way he took in the icy pond convinced me I was alone. I trudged ahead. The car couldn't be far away.

# The Empty House

*IT'S BEEN A COUPLE OF MONTHS NOW,* I SAID. *I NEED TO find a job or I'll have to move.* The windows along the main room of The Apartment were open. There wasn't any wind.

*Yeah I'm sure you're gonna find a job on a Friday,* Star said over the phone. *Just come down.*

I never packed for Corinna's. I could always borrow clothes from Paul if I needed them, and why would I need them? I didn't even listen to music on the way there, just kept the windows down and soaked in the quiet when I slowed for tolls. There was barely any traffic and it wasn't close to dark when I pulled up in front of Corinna's. I liked the feeling of walking away from the car empty-handed, convincing myself I smelled the ocean.

I unlatched the back gate and walked into the yard. Star was there. She could fall asleep instantly and I guessed she was sleeping now, facedown on the lounge chair by the glass door. She wore only the low part of her swimsuit; she must have been trying to tan. Her top didn't seem to be around the lounge chair, which had to mean Corinna's mother was gone. I slipped off my boots and socks and left them in the crabgrass. Barefoot, I crept to the pool and scooped a little water. Star looked up just as I started to rush her. She'd been awake.

"Drop it! Put your hands down now! Jack!" She shouted and rose up to kneeling, covering her chest. "Put the water down, Jack!"

What would have been fun with Corinna felt cruel with Star. I ran my wet hands through my hair.

Star blushed to the top of her chest. "Give me something," she said, looking around for a towel or a shirt. There wasn't anything so I thumbed the shirt collar at the back of my neck and slipped it over my head.

Star covered herself with an arm and reached out. I turned away: Victorian roofs were visible over the fence, the blue shades next door rolled up.

"That's where the poet lives," she said.

"You mean Charles Jodoin?"

"The one Corinna's dad used to know." She was latching the buttons as I turned back.

"Are they here?" I asked, meaning Paul and Corinna.

"Paul had some clambake he wanted to go to," she said. "That Ronan guy he works for. Corinna said she wanted to meet him, so they're gone."

I didn't like the thought of Corinna networking with Paul, meeting married lawnmower couples, laughing stories. I pictured a bonfire, paper plates. I'd never been at the house without Corinna.

"Have you ever been to the basement?" I asked

Star, moving toward the glass doors.

"Are you going down there?" she asked. But I was already pulled by a heady urge through the open glass door and into the dark living room.

Corinna gone, I wanted to search the house. On the far side of the room, I pushed the flat door by the fireplace and, when it gave, got a faceful of must. There was dust on the light switch when I flicked it. The unfinished wooden steps at my feet seemed like an architectural afterthought as I clomped down, feeling them shake with disuse, and into the vault of gray stone and concrete arches.

"What do you want to do down here?" Star asked, her mouth unhappy. I hadn't felt her on the stairs behind me.

"Have you been down here?" I asked, moving toward what I later realized was a dusty, unused loom by the foot of the stairs.

"High school," she said. "Corinna and I used to smoke pot down here while her mom was asleep." She sounded embarrassed.

"I'd think...well, why wouldn't you do that in the attic? I mean, smoke rises."

"Shut up. Yeah, we got caught."

"Corinna's mom?"

"Yeah, she was cool, but I guess she mentioned it to Corinna's dad a few days later and you know how he was."

"Not really," I said. "I met you guys after he left..."

"He was insane. Stupid Republican crazy."

"I didn't…"

"No one talks about him because he's dead. But Corinna called me a week after we found out her mom had smelled us in the basement. I came over. Her dad was there and seriously it was like being in the room with the president. I mean he sat there in his chair."

"You mean Paul's chair?"

"And he said *You need to think about growing up* or something. He had this mustache. It was small, though. He trimmed it so it didn't grow in the middle. He had this way of talking like you could tell he thought he was being really indulgent."

"You mean like in that divot under your nose?"

"Yeah, exactly. Like wherever the Hitler mustache was growing he didn't want a mustache."

"I never heard he was a Republican."

"Well he acted like one." She wandered to a stack of moldy boxes. "These are all filled with his art books, I guess. Corinna was saying her mom was gonna sell them to help move, but I wouldn't want to buy them."

I walked over to one of the boxes and peeled open a flap through the tape. The cardboard tore soft as orange peel. Inside were what looked like unbound pages of a black and white book of art history. The art was Indian: wild-armed Vishnus and fat, happy Ganeshes like Buddhas.

I pictured Bill down there with Corinna, moving among the lakes of paper that would have waited in dry stacked beds four or so years ago. I couldn't picture him looking inside. Corinna would have been nervous around him, a way she never was with Paul.

"Bill showed me a book of Native American art the old man gave him," I said. "It was in the same series."

"Are you guys gonna put a rain dance in your play?"

"Snow dance. The play died last winter."

Star leaned against me in the silk shirt while I paged through the Hindu art. I couldn't imagine believing in the cosmic system the androgynous, blue-skinned Krishnas held, hands poised, with wheels and shells like grenades with invisible pins.

"Did you ever meditate with Bill in his closet?" Star asked, the itch of her hair on my cheek.

"Is that what you guys call it?" Her fingers were red. I noticed she'd rested a few on the hand I held the book in. "When are they coming back from their cookout?"

"I don't know," she said. "It's a day thing, so I guess they won't all freak out like they did last time."

"What do you mean?" I shut the book and dropped it in the box.

"They were dancing. Paul wanted to escape."

"Calling the universe to order?"

She started back upstairs, so I followed her.

"Salsa. Have you heard of that? It's something people do."

"Yeah. But Paul can't."

"Paul was smiling like this." She stopped at the foot of the stairs and squinted suave. "And then he was like—" she opened her eyes wide, darted them around. In her rare impersonations Star moved more quickly then the person she was being ever could. I liked them though, and they were funny to me because they always most reminded me of Star.

The second I started grinning she was laughing. We ran up the stairs and into the glassed-in living room.

"Hello!" I shouted.

"You wanna explore the upstairs?" She was excited.

"Uh, let's go for a walk." I wanted to go down to the breakwaters.

"Okay. Corinna said you almost killed everyone out there on the Fourth."

"Yeah," I said, stepping into the white sun of the patio, pulling my cigarettes out of my jeans. "Paul crooked them into the rock wrong." I thought about asking for one of the art books. Maybe the one she'd given Bill.

"Oh, Paul did?" she said, taking the cigarette out of my fingers. "Corinna said it was you."

# Spilled Gin

ONE WEEK INTO AUGUST, JUST TWO WEEKS BEFORE Charles Jodoin's big end-of-summer lawn party, Corinna came by herself to The Apartment. Paul was "too busy with the mid-summer rush" (if he didn't move lawnmowers now, he wouldn't be able to—the year was closing down). I picked her up at South Station and we walked our way across the city, stopping at a basement noodle place on Newbury.

"Star's going to some camping thing with Mara," she said.

"Just the two of them?"

"Oh!" Corinna waved her hands. "It's some festival thing where they roll around in mud and listen to music."

"But they'll get all *dirty*," I said.

She smiled wide. "Like Mara isn't dirty enough already! Smelly, nasty cunt!"

"Dripping, evil cunt." Corinna liked the game and I was happy to play.

We both ordered sweet buckwheat noodles, laughing about how long it took us to decide. She made a show out of not being able to eat them with the chopsticks. I wouldn't usually have thought it was so funny, but I was nerved up from us being alone.

I made up the pull-out couch when we got home. Before she met Paul, it was a given that Corinna would sleep curled around me in my narrow twin. Since then, they always came up together and shared the pull-out, but now I wasn't sure what the arrangement was. Neither of us were, I could tell by the slow way we got ready.

I waited until she changed into her camisole and crawled in. Then, after I turned the lights off, I slipped into the cool sheets. She didn't move, and she and I lay still on our backs, as though we'd sleep like that. Through the open window, we took in the sound of bars closing down and a few of the lonely hollers you get in the Back Bay, and the steady wind. She told me a story about trying to go camping with Bill in high school, how they got too cold in their tent and drove all the way home in the middle of the night. I talked too, not moving, not wanting to shift the way I naturally would. She didn't turn to look at me, though, not without telling some story she pretended to be excited about.

I woke up with my back to her. It was the first time we'd shared a bed without touching. I could feel her wake up behind me, half wake up. She could have stretched, crawled out, started the hot water, but she didn't. Anything I did would be the wrong thing.

We each pretended we didn't know the other was

fully awake. She lifted her arm behind me, stiffly, and let it fall on my chest. She'd given up muscle control, let's say, her arm just lay there.

What could I do? I rolled onto my back the way I would half asleep, wrapping into her free arm, letting it turn to touch my chin.

And she pulled up to me, pressing the bridge of her nose into my neck. I barely felt her breath.

There was no way I could win. I lifted my arm and she buried her head in my chest, the way she used to. With a flick, I lifted her camisole beneath the sheets, set my hand on her warm skin, buried it along where her belly sloped.

She'd been awake, like I knew she was, and she bit my earlobe, laughing to herself. Hard. I moved my hand, enjoying the feel, up to her breast. I cupped her in my palm. I pulled her down to kiss me. And she did, hard again, but laughing through it, like it was a game.

Then she got up, long legs flashing out of bed, and made us tea.

Jump forward one week. Me drinking the same tea in her kitchen. Her across from me, boxers and camisole. Paul still out.

"What's he doing?" I asked. "He should have been home two hours ago."

"He drives around."

He drinks. "How's the lawnmower business?"

She lifted the camisole to scratch her ribs, as though she didn't know how I'd feel. "He…"

The secrets of marriage, the private fire. Bugs

thumped into the narrow kitchen window. We were both full of milky caffeine and talking, but I'd almost quit trying to win her over. I let myself go.

"Boston is so perfect for you," she said. "All those old writers, and little bookstores and coffee shops."

"Yeah," I said, "but where are the poets? I feel like I'm looking for them, but it seems like, you know, I go to acting class where he has us pretend to be furniture, then I walk around and I go back to The Apartment in the evening and it's basically like I'm commuting to Nowhereland every night. You won't introduce me to Charles Jodoin. There's Bill, but he lives in New York."

"Yeah!" she said, trying, "you're Maybe the May-which."

Corinna stopped and listened. A second later I heard Paul pull into the gravel drive. We were quiet while he opened the front door and dropped his case in the hall, both of us surprised by how drunk he looked as he walked into the library with a half-empty fifth of Sapphire.

*"I've been out with Ronan."*

Corinna and I didn't speak. We were pure audience.

*"Neither of you want to talk to me, right! You want to talk to one another! You can be that!"*

An instant later, once he was asleep on the couch, with the half-empty bottle balanced on his chest, Corinna and I moved from the table to the doorway and watched him. I put my hand in her back pocket. She followed me.

"When we…were living together…me and Paul…I'd…he'd snore, and…"

Paul wasn't a person but a joke on the couch. I smelled the top of Corinna's head, inhaling worlds. She let me.

"I would take little pieces of Kleenex and put them just under his nose. And he'd whiff 'em and turn over."

She opened her mouth to giggle. I shushed her and, like always, I cupped her ass, murmured shusshhhh. I felt her wrestle against me. Her arm fell around my waist.

"That would wake him up?" She whispered in my ear, sound diffused.

"Oh yeah."

I waited to see if she'd move her hand. She did, a little, then said, "We've got some Kleenex in the Buddha room."

It was awkward to move through the kitchen and computer room with my arm around her, but we managed it. Her father had been on various trips to Laos, Cambodia. He was too old for the war, and she never explained what an art publisher was doing out so far in the seventies — there were no Cambodian books on the shelf — but his small collection of Buddhas was impressive enough to fill an annex off the computer room, its own annex off the den.

I said, "You know, the MFA has a Buddha room."

"You go there to meditate?" Her breath on my neck.

"I tried…" I said.

"Yeah, it's not your thing," she said. "Checking your hair in the, um, mahogany polishing."

"Fuck you. Where's the…"

"There."

"Ah ha, ha ha."

I took a single Kleenex back to the library. She came up next to me, watching as I crept exaggeratedly up to Paul, bottle open on his chest, and placed it above his mouth. The touch opened his eyes—not on me, on the ceiling—and he shouted startled as he sat upright, not seeing the gin, spilling it all over his white shirt and tie, darkening his heaving chest. It was more like a growl then a shout and it echoed in my ear. I'd backed into the hall corner by then. He reached out to grab the bottle but batted it into the air instead. I already felt guilty at how wildly apart he seemed and how desperate he was not to spill any more. Corinna laughed at him, shouting, "The couch, you're getting it all over…"

He didn't know where he was. I felt cruel, worse than I should have felt. I walked over to grab the bottle but he glared straight through me. Then he was standing up, covered in gin from his neck to his waist, his tie was dark with it. I could smell it where I was standing by the door, astringently strong as he pushed past me on the way out, drunkenly opening his wet shirt.

Corinna looked as though she couldn't decide whether to laugh or worry. Then she saw the bottle balanced on one of the cushions.

"Oh, God, it'll spill!"

I was closer so I grabbed it. There was a quarter inch left.

"Is your mom going to be worried about the couch?"

We surveyed the impact. The lower cushions were moist.

"It all ended up on my husband."

"He saved that sofa."

Corinna disappeared into the kitchen while I pulled the pillow up to see if it was double-sided so that maybe I could reverse it.

"Where did the stain go?" She put a bottle of tequila, two glasses, and a lime on the coffee table.

"I hid it. Worst case, Paul can pay for cleaning."

"Um, sweetie. Well, I don't know…"

"What?"

She went back to the kitchen for salt. We hadn't drunk alone with one another in what felt like years. She poured two glasses of the tequila—"It's all we have in the house"—and cut the lime into wedges.

"Has Paul…talked to you much about the lawn-mowers? I mean, I'm sure he has, but I mean has he told you about how the sales are going?"

I drank back a shot and we sucked the limes.

"Are you telling me there isn't a trapdoor filled with money?"

"I wish…Paul hasn't…there's only one lawn-mower he's sold so far, and it's to us."

"He bought it?"

"My mom did. It cost her a thousand dollars."

"Jesus. You guys don't have a lawn even."

"Yeah, tell me about it."

"This is a *town*house."

What looked like long-legged mosquitoes climbed the walls around us, butted against the ceiling. She poured another drink, mine filled higher then hers so I took the bottle and tipped both shots to the rim.

"Hey!"

I pulled the hand from her wet glass and turned it over, poured a little salt on the inside of her wrist and licked it off. She licked the rest and back went the shots.

"Look at this!" I said. "He's going to come downstairs and be all, *I'm sorry for drinking so much.*"

She tipped her head back and laughed sharp to the ceiling.

"Yeah!" she said. "Who's the filthy drunk now?"

I looked around the library and for a second the books just looked like books, blocks…something that wasn't worth caring about.

"It must be wonderful," I said, at the instant I quit seeing it, "living here with all this stuff that predates you, the Buddhas, you know, but the books too. And all those art books you guys have in the basement, those boxes of them."

She poured another shot and drank it without waiting for our tiny ceremony. The inside of her wrist must have still been salty.

"Yeah, um, it's frightening, actually," she said.

"The evil Buddhas?"

"Yeah. No, really. When Paul's out selling lawn-mowers."

"Or not selling them."

"I don't want to think about it. I just…it gets scary here all alone."

"You think that famous poet's going to come over here and molest you?"

"Um, I think he'd be more likely to molest you, sweetie."

"Well," I said, taking a drink from the bottle to impress her, even though she didn't look impressed, "I'm here to protect you."

"Protect me from my husband? What?"

"You'll have to protect me from him, probably." It was the wrong note and we both knew it. I lit a Zodiak.

"Let me taste that," she said, reaching for it. "Oh my god!" Her cheeks puffed up and she made a show out of coughing. "Those are like poison."

"We poets," I said blustery, touching my chest with my fist, "have poison in our hearts!"

She smiled. "Oh, are you trying to be Bill now?"

"Bill Lite," I said, meaning it.

"Oh my god, you totally are! Wow, I am really drunk!"

"Probably Bill's drunk too."

"Yeah," she said, pouring a little tequila in her glass and not drinking it. "Fucking some dirty actress in New York."

"He had some new girl, last I talked to him. Some rich girl from Long Island. He said they used to fuck on her father's private yacht. And he could feel the ocean. Said…"

"Okay, enough!" She looked haggard, "Do you guys tell each other everything?"

"Used to," I said. "We haven't talked since this winter."

"Really?" She squinted when she was drunk. "I thought you guys were tight."

# Birdlike

I'd been listening to Sibelius on headphones, navigating my tequila hangover to acting class when I felt a strange hand grab my arm. I'd passed Toby's apartment a block back so he must have been walking behind me.

I jumped, spun around, the fact that I was back in Boston came across in the blare of cars. The erotic cake shop confronted me. I realized that Toby hadn't meant to startle me and that he was talking.

"Sorry, Toby."

"You were finding your space?" he asked, impersonating our professor CB's voice. CB spoke soothingly during class, even spaces between his words, and Toby did him expertly, leaning in on *space*.

"*Yes*," I said, happy to joke back, frowning my eyes while I smiled, which was CB's way of telling us we were amateurs, although I'd never seen CB look at Toby that way.

"I've been going down to Rhode Island on the weekends," I told him, opening up, walking again, wiping sweat off my face, "next one too. There's this big party at a poet's house. Ever hear of Charles Jodoin?"

"Is he a poet? I should read poetry." He didn't sound ambitious.

I stopped at my favorite Bassett hound's backyard at the corner of Essex. She was happy to see me and I bent to rub her ears through the low iron fence. There was a hundred-year-old basement on her breath.

"How's *Unfinished*?" I asked him. *Unfinished* was Toby's directorial thesis, a bunch of scenes from various unfinished plays performed by some actors with no interruptions, scene breaks, or announced transitions. He was accepting bits of plays from anyone.

"You know Bill Brennan?" Toby asked.

"Bill?"

"He mentioned you, said I might know you from school."

"He asked about me?" I felt excited for a second, then remembered we weren't talking.

"I think it was you." He let the dog sniff his hand but he didn't pet her. "We're gonna take the potential last scene from *Sacred Sin*."

"*Sacred Sin*?"

"He sent us this scene, it's about a high-school girl and a Pequot Warrior. And I don't know how to explain it, but she *is* the Indian. He's her untamed side. Her *Sheut*."

"Shoot?"

"The Egyptians believed in your *Sheut*." Toby lit into it. "Like her shadow—it accompanies her everywhere. And there's this boy she's in love with awakening a womanly, a mature side of her. It's '50s styled, Patsy Cline. And so she has to kill the Native American, this tomboy side of her, her *Sheut*. So that she can finally grow up, raise a kid. And it's really good for the festival because, you know, there's just these four characters and lots of poetry and no real set. She and the Indian are gonna fight for possession of her soul and her body and the Indian's gonna end up killing her boyfriend. That's our scene: she and her boyfriend load her dad's house with dynamite but the Indian *sheut* escapes and explodes it with her boyfriend inside. Then he separates from her soul while she speeds away."

Why was it so hot so early? I heard the cars going by on my left and their sounds were like final straws — each seemed to push me farther into the future and I didn't want to go.

"It's poetry," Toby said, "'*His tears can make a forest for Dakota. At his small words acres smolder.*' It's beautiful."

I remembered that I'd told Bill about Toby's project over the phone. "We're gonna be late," I said. I didn't know where Bill lived anymore. "We're not gonna get the chance to, uh, impersonate objects in class, be the breeze, learn to breathe."

"I'm sure they're still stretching," Toby said as we turned the last block.

"Let it all loose," I half-imitated CB again, sibilating my esses, rolling my shoulders, hoping Toby would quit talking about Bill, get into the spirit of it.

It worked: Toby stopped still, let his studded jacket slip half off his shoulders and his hands retreated in his sleeves. He let his stomach go and kept his palms pressed like prayer. He said, "Hmmmm." Thoughtful, suspicious, perfectly CB. It was eerie, right down to CB's one-leg-poised *physical articulation*.

We hopped up the steps, walked through the big main stage room, and into a back annex room of the Neshoba Theater, CB's hands up his sleeves.

"Let's make a circle," CB said, and Toby and I slipped off our jackets and quietly circled with the group. Never in Boston on the weekends, I hadn't drunk or stayed out late with the class and I didn't know them well. They were all beautiful, none of the girls made up, everyone in sweats or shorts, wife-beaters. I exchanged a couple of smiles—usually a beat late—and I found my place. Everyone looked down at the mats on the floor, embarrassed to stare at one another, or seeming that way.

I focused on Julie. We'd had coffee once and she told me she used to be a dancer. Her posture was like Corinna's: tight and relaxed, like a soldier at ease when the war's okay.

I wound up standing straight across from CB. "What I want you to do today," he said, looking at me but talking to everyone, "is pick a gesture. It doesn't matter what gesture it is. You can move your arm, wave…it doesn't matter exactly…" (palms to his mouth) "what."

A loud-voiced girl named Sonya made a show of

smoothing her long black hair. She looked around. At CB's nod she smoothed it theatrically.

"Everybody," he repeated, "gesture, repeat it, and let it be natural."

I tried to feel whatever I was feeling. I found myself turning my palms up by my sides, letting them drop back down. Toby stared ahead, then started patting his pocket for his wallet and keys. Next to me, Julie put her hands on her hips and huffed her chest.

"Everyone have one? Good. Now. Walk with it. That's right, just walk around the room." We began to walk. "Now... *exaggerate* that gesture."

Toby started bugging his eyes when he checked for his wallet. There was a shortish boy on the periphery whose cigarette mime became effeminate. Surprising to me, my palm-up I-dunno grew aggressive, like a barked *what* before the start of a fight, but silent—an affront that was all in my arms.

"Good, keep exaggerating. *Be* that gesture."

For some reason, this started us looking one another in the eye. Sonya frisked her hair back, staring at me, and I barked a *what* with my hands. Julie strutted, tilting up her chin. My *what* hands reached wider and higher. The way it felt to make the gesture changed and I started to imagine myself angrily conducting a symphony, one that could clash on without me.

CB retreated to a corner, exaggerating the relaxation of his walk. His voice, when it came, was a touch loud.

"There is an animal inside your gestures. There is an animal inside your gesture Toby, can you find him?"

Starting with Toby was smart. He unblinkingly shifted his paranoid patting into a cross between a scratch and a primp. Holding his hands extended like a nimble, bottom-heavy raccoon, he began to "wash some food." He continued to walk around the room, only this time with a careful waddle.

"Julie," CB said, "where is your animal? You've got to find your animal, Julie. Jack, what is your animal doing? What does he want to do?"

As in each class, there was a point at which the smell of sweat and the coffee on everyone's breath overpowered the sawdust smell. I caught it as we made a play jungle, growling and cawing. I believe Sonya was a fierce cat attempting to eat Toby's raccoon. We all smelled human.

"Now behave in a way that is true to how your animal behaves," CB shouted, "if your animal is a predator, stalk your prey. If you are their prey, run."

A blond boy rolled himself into a ball on the ground. Sonya poked him with her nose before stalking on. Julie was a peacock, frisking away from predators, preening.

I was high up and flying. The *what* in my arms spread full length and straight out, perpendicular. I relaxed and snapped my elbows, glided over the room. My eyes may have been malevolent, but I felt myself at a huge remove. Even CB was small.

We looked at one another in equipoise. And it was him who looked away.

I can't say that I didn't want to roll on the floor in my sweatpants with them all, but it didn't feel like my place.

While CB shouted, "The sun is getting low…you haven't eaten yet!" I flew around the room twice, keeping my eyes up at the high wall sconces and gargoyle boss. I pushed the air out with my palms, then dropped them to sweep it. The violence of the push was only appropriate to what it takes to stay aloft in the air, not the big swipe it takes to lift off the ground.

Small birds retract their wings to rise. I pushed mine out. I left the stage and lifted over the velvet seats of the wing with *I Folle* written in the wain-scot, the worn red seats tucked-and-sprung to the seatbacks. I hung midair a foot below the arched ceiling, feeling the full potential of the theater seats until I felt their emptiness. I pushed through the back doors of the tech box and into the empty lob-by and circled twice onto the dirty floor.

Outside, human, I walked quickly and easily home down the green strip of a garden on Commonwealth Ave, anxious to get to my car, drive down to the shore and wait for Corinna's second boat of the day to arrive back. All efficiency, she'd be checking the rigging in her cutoffs and her sweater. She'd see me with surprise and charge off and into me.

I'd ride the next tour out with her, fill her up with the story, let her laugh in my ear.

# The Captain's Table

"Pull over there," Bill said. We'd passed the Arby's.

"You don't want…"

"I don't know what I want. I want some kind of *thing*…"

He grabbed up with his fingers balletically, meaning he wanted something cheese-covered.

"I want a *thing* too, but *there* it is."

The Captain's Table hollered out at us around one of Route Two's slow bends. You never know where the entrance drive is, pick the wrong one, and you've got to park at a decaying strip club or a castle of Boston-themed plush lobsters.

Inside, we opened the enormous menus, flipped through the cardboard pages. I looked across the salt shakers at Bill who was sitting sideways in the booth, head in his hand. "Everything has cheese on it. We should get the biggest thing."

"When's the last time you ate?"

He moved his fingers while he counted backward.

"New York."

"Was that yesterday?"

"Was it two days ago?"

I stared out the window at the late-winter light, unsure if I felt alright or if I was unknowingly on the cusp of exhaustion.

"Was it earlier today?"

He laughed. "How are we going to write a play?"

"Did you put the typewriter in the car?"

"You did."

We were close, but I always wanted to be closer. It was the same with Corinna.

"And here we are," I said. "Sitting around high. Corinna's married."

"You're thinking about her."

"No," I said. I was remembering, for the first time in a long while, running into them both, having seen them around. I'd felt alive that day, sixteen years old with the car to myself, I'd driven to the beach where my grandparents used to live, where I'd kissed a girl I barely knew a few weeks earlier. I stripped down and jumped in, driving barefoot back to town, long hair dry with salt, sand in my cuffs. I saw them leaning on the brand new Vietnam memorial in the park, smoking. I'd met them once or twice, but we hadn't talked. Bill had only showed up a few months earlier and he already had the best girl. She was one of the few of us with old money, even if it wasn't from our town.

I had parked and walked up to them barefoot. She was dressed in one of his torn shirts, her arms drawn inside it. He wore a lacrosse shirt with only the top button done.

I had asked him what he was reading.

"Is Paul…" Bill leaned over the menu, "working, or…?"

"Or. Yeah. It's no fun coming down."

"To see them?"

"No I mean coming down from the drugs."

Bill scowled because the waitress for our table might have heard me. It never bothered me to talk about what I'd taken; my thinking was that people talked about drinking and drugs all the time, and not when they were drunk and high or loudly making fun of the kind of people who did that sort of thing.

"You guys need a couple more minutes?"

She was sixteen, if that, red-haired like Bill, pale, but the style of speech was stolen from a forty-year veteran. She'd been watching someone.

"No," Bill said, his command returned. "I'll have the family-size fettuccini alfredo."

"Two. And can we get a big plate of cheese fries?" I nearly said, "And a bottle of wine," but it had been two straight days of self-abuse and enough was enough.

"Water. Big one."

I dumped the last two cigarettes on the table and lit one even though I didn't feel like smoking it.

"You know what you haven't said anything about," I prodded. "Your girl on Long Island. You were all excited about her…" I was trying to make conversation and it was obvious. Bill had a changing but fiery grip on what he held sacred.

He stared. "Don't say anything too much about her. I mean, you don't know who knows who. You like to talk."

"I don't even know her name. What? She have a boyfriend?"

Bill nodded slow.

"Well I hear you," I said.

"Someone," he asked, the girl putting water on the table, "new?"

I shook my head, fixed on the floating lemon.

"Her."

"Alright."

"What?"

"There's something wrong with you, Jack."

"I'm just in love."

"No. You want to win. You want to beat Paul. It's all about a contest."

"Where…"

Our waitress laid a white platter of cheese fries between us. Whole peppers were sliced up under the cheese. And colonies of chopped tomato. And massacred beef.

"We'll get back to that," I said. "Let me just…"

"Sure."

We ate fast, pulling at the wet fries. I liked it best when a salty chunk would lift a flat of cheese off a naked cluster. We dug the rim-hardened cheese with our nails and ate the flakes.

Bill sat back exhausted. His throat was pale. His soul had left.

"You don't tell me enough about your life," I said.

"I know I just feel…"

"You're upset about the Corinna thing."

He didn't say *Find your own life, Jack*, but he could have. Except that he and Corinna were my life. I was the one who wanted to come into theirs, the thought to stop by the monument, the sepia rush. I still wanted it, between them and the monument, between each other.

"Here you are…hon'."

Thin arms trembling with the weight, she set the platters of fettuccini down. Lines of it crept around the building-sized wedges of green and red pepper. The sauce was already salt crystal. The noodles were white and dry yellow and the cheese on top hardened.

Twenty minutes later, when it was clear we weren't going to eat more than a bite or two, we paid, walked out in the dark, toward the car. With the typewriter tugging at the back of my mind, I glanced in the back seat. There was nothing there. Instinctively, I tried the doors. They were locked. No one had taken it.

"We left the typewriter."

"We *what?* Look!"

We checked under the seats, in the trunk. We checked everything twice.

"When do you have to get back to New York?"

"I have to sleep."

"Sleep in…can you sleep in the car?"

Bill's eyes searched the parking lot and their light retreated inside him. He wanted to be angry but he didn't know how best to do it. So he shrugged down quiet in his seat and didn't talk until we'd crossed into Concord in the dark.

# The Open Field

WE COULD ALREADY HEAR CARS ARRIVING AT THE blue house as we waited for Star by the pool, Corinna in khaki shorts and a tank top, Paul in his usual linen. I was warm in black jeans and boots. Sweat dripped under my shirt.

Paul asked, "Do you want a drink before we go over?"

"As soon as Star gets here," I said. "Let's not start without her."

"Look at you, looking out for Star," Corinna said. "Don't you think Jack and Star would make a good couple?"

"Isn't Star already with Mara?" Paul asked. "Think you can handle both of them, Jack?"

"I'm not entirely sure," I said, drawing it out, "that Mara is a human woman."

"Give it up, Jack," Corinna said. "We know you like those little suicidal girls with the big noses. Like back in high school. All Jack's girls were like Wednesday Addams."

"Then you wouldn't be my type."

"I thought Paul was your type." She laughed, looked happy. "Maybe you two can make out next door and impress those guys at the party."

"No," Paul said.

I felt a touch on the shoulder. It was Star, wearing the black silk shirt I'd loaned her the afternoon we'd explored the basement. I liked the idea of her wearing something of mine. I always like that.

"Mara couldn't come," Star said. "She's having some thing tomorrow night and she wants to sleep. So can I get…"

"I'll give you a ride home. I don't want to stay too late." So I was with Star.

"Great, me neither. Are you all still smoking? Jesus, you guys are gonna kill all the birds."

"Oh? I thought Mara smoked," Corinna said.

"Yeah," Star said, waving the smoke away, exaggeratedly relaxing on a lawn chair, "but I don't get it from all sides."

"So," Corinna said, "I was telling Jack he should give his play to Charles Jodoin."

"Jack doesn't have a play," Star said, uncurling her legs on the long chair, letting her arms hang.

"Yes you do." Corinna asked me, "Didn't you and Bill start one last winter?"

An airplane tracked under a cloud and we heard the hum. I tried to feel as though Paul was an impediment who could get scratched away, the pool and the house mine, backyard hot in the sun. But I couldn't make the vision accumulate and I felt the prick of *You don't live in their world*.

Paul got up and came back a minute later with cool gin and tonics mixed with lots of squeezed lime. Corinna drained hers thirstily. I sipped a little, mostly wanting water but not getting up.

"Yeah, the plot's about this…girl on a train. She's going away to school. And she has this kind of shady father figure. Her real father died years ago and he was friendly with her mother."

"Friendly?" Star said, "or…"

"Well," I said, "we're not really sure. Bill doesn't like the idea of the old guy at all."

"What's it about?" Corinna was listening. Paul wasn't.

"Well," I said, "Bill and I don't talk like we used to."

"Well maybe he doesn't want to write about people who aren't from New York. He did move away from here and all."

"Well," I said, "I moved up to Boston."

"Yeah, sweetie, that's why you're here." If she were the kind of person who winked, she would have.

"David wants to talk," Paul said with pride, "about maybe having me check in on the house over the fall, when they're away."

"Don't they have Rosita the Spanish maid or something?" Corinna asked. "People go in and out of there."

Paul flicked his cigarette, hand palm up, said, "Maybe…" and then he got drowned out by Star who was up and moving around, leaning down, whispering, "Come in the kitchen."

"Mara saw Paul the other day." We stood by the

over-crammed tea cupboard. I heard Corinna run for the phone upstairs. Somewhere outside, Paul probably finished his drink.

"Okay."

"I guess Paul's worried."

Star was standing closer these days; I felt the tips of her breasts when she leaned up to whisper.

"I told Mara that Paul didn't have to care, that you were over the whole Corinna thing."

"There isn't a thing."

"That's what I told her."

"But what…" I sat on the kitchen chair and patted my lap. "What exactly did Mara say Paul was worried about?" I wanted to hear my name.

Star smiled and sat on my lap. I petted the back of her hair which made her move closer. "You really want to talk about it?"

"You brought it up." I took my hand away and sat back. "What did Paul say?"

"That he thinks Corinna's screwing around."

"Oh. What did Mara say?"

Star rolled her eyes. "Mara said what everyone says, that she thinks you want to sleep with Corinna but you haven't."

"Why does she think I haven't? Wait a minute, she only knows what you tell her, why would you think I…"

"Oh, please, Jack. Do you think you would have slept with her and not told me?"

"Hey! But, wait, how did Paul end up talking to Mara?"

"Jack!" She ran a hand through my hair. "He goes door to door with those things."

I guessed Charles Jodoin and David didn't need one of Paul's lawnmowers. The grass on their lawn was trim, but not in the military crew style of Paul's pamphlets. It seemed contoured, shorter in stylized patches, as though it were cut with a razor.

Unlike Corinna's overgrown garden and antique swimming pool Jodoin's backyard was carefully tended: rows of flowers in a careful zig along the high stone wall, a long slope up to the house. And unlike Corinna's, it wasn't a townhouse, thanks to the empty, manicured lots the wall held. The house joined the wall streetside, and we had to walk in the front door and through a handful of big rooms to reach the crowd out back.

David opened the door. The same man Paul had talked to with deference outside Ricky Bang-Bang's, he held himself like, in a Charles Jodoin line, an *old libertine who'd learned how to shudder.* There was a worn-in quality to David that matched his surroundings. It could have been Corinna's house, same floor plan, the front door opening on a main staircase with rooms to the left and right, connected without hallways, without doors, rooms opening on rooms through slight constrictions in the walls, small windows throughout until the glass patio doors opened on the wide lawn.

There were photographs everywhere, matted on the walls and framed on the tables. Famous poets with Charles Jodoin. David rattled a routine hello, "…drinks in the kitchen and outside, god! Help yourself make yourself at home…" He disappeared as we stepped into the sun.

I turned on my bluster.

"Y'all want a drink? Corinna! I'm ashamed at your not drinking. I'm going to fill you up with something. Star. Star? What'll it be?" I touched her chin with Paul and Corinna looking on. I ordered four drinks at the long, catered table, directed their mix (a "Walden Pond": Diet Coke, vodka, lime, sugared rim).

Paul was already off, pulling Corinna after him. The lawn was rich with old timers, local business owners and small politicians from the newspapers, most of them over fifty, one glittering exception in the young go-getter with his pretty young wife.

"Jesus, Jack, they're just people talking."

"Am I talking out loud? Well that's my first mistake tonight." I leaned in when I said it but it wasn't a good line. Star was comfortable. She'd spent every weekend with Corinna in high school, at least the ones Corinna didn't spend with Bill, so she knew some of the faces here. She recognized one as an old dance teacher.

"Mr. Milldan!"

He looked blank at first, but even I can see Star's changed. Corinna had always been a year older, fixing Star's clothes (hand-me-downs of Corinna's, worn rolled up or tied at the waist, or rip-offs), her social associations. Mr. Milldan looked at her confused. Clearly, she was one of his students, but who had he taught with six linked rings in her ear, or a star tattoo below it? Then he must have seen her eyes, the clever sparks on the surface, the deep.

"Star!" He pointed at the new tattoo and laughed. Then he smiled like they were old friends, older than she and I were. I scanned the rest of the lawn for Paul and Corinna but they were lost in the summer shirts.

I was surprised by the even mix of locals, the wide range in age from thirty-five to eighty. What had I been expecting? A yard full of artists, where I would be taken in, instead of standing there with my face pressed on the glass?

I wandered, always fixing an object a few meters off and walking toward it, turning and rejudging. I held the pack of Zodiaks in my right hand, thinking someone — maybe Charles Jodoin — might ask for one.

Gradually, I wound my way back to Star, who was talking with both Mr. Milldan and, presumably, his wife.

"Oh, she was always like that, remember that face…"

"Star," I said, tapping her shoulder, "I'm going to look around in the house. If you're looking for me. Okay?"

She looked at me as if she weren't really sure of why I was telling her this, but she touched my arm anyway. I moved toward the house thinking if I was stopped, I'd say I wanted a bathroom. Mostly,

I wanted to see the library, find the poet.

I put out my Zodiak before I walked out of the sun into the comparatively dim kitchen, but felt foolish for doing it when I saw David smoking at the table, explaining something to Paul.

"Where's Corinna?" I asked.

Paul heard me and looked away.

"Paul? Where's Corinna?" I got a little closer and saw that David was gesturing at a checklist. I thought of the advantage, coming along with Paul on trips to check the place out, sweeping the drawers in the poet's study for letters from even more famous poets, his own unpublished stuff. I'd barely scratched the stuff I bought at the bookstore, but unpublished work is more intimate.

I got close enough that David looked up at me. Paul had to answer.

"She's with Star."

David smiled at me, throwing a shine in his eye. So I was Paul's friend?

"Where's the bathroom?"

David pointed and gave me a lot of exaggerated directions, joking about the outline of the house, the quirky furniture, imagined mess. It was well-delivered, if rehearsed, but I mostly snuck looks at the checklist he'd been explaining to Paul, smiled at TEND TO LAWN.

Elizabeth Bishop seemed dazed in the silver frame by the den couch. She held a big, dead fish at arm's length, as though she'd drop it the instant the shutter snapped. Small on the mantle, Robert

Lowell's stubble was badly shaved. Already, I felt like an eavesdropper, falling back on the lost sense of being watched, feeling myself alone.

In Corinna's house the library bordered the kitchen. Since her father died they'd used it for a living room, smelling it up with cheese, moving in a TV. Here, though, there was no library, at least not one I could find on the ground floor. Turning, I put my foot on the first stair. It creaked loud but I crept up quiet as I could. Corinna's house felt more lived in, but Charles and David were only here for the summer, and they were only two people. They didn't have Star, or me, creeping through the space, augmenting and bullying. I imagined my history in Corinna's house, moving from room to room. I thought of what Corinna and Paul must feel, hearing my steps on the old wood from where they slept, feeling the tug between the friend I was and the friend they wanted: the visible extension of themselves.

> What children do, as children say,
> is confiscated by
> another wall, the play
> our play, imploring
> STAY, through windows…

A few of the Jodoin lines I knew moved. I didn't understand why he used capital letters but they made the page hum. It was a voice he heard from somewhere maybe, some cold command.

I said I'LL COME TO YOU,
But David stumbled in with drinks,
Drowned your voice. The call
Of stranded children couldn't catch

That hundred year old gaze
TO SEA where a man like me
If ancient, shaped like me if gone
Met China's gold. I raise your....

There were old, framed maps at the top landing and two divergent paths down a gray carpet to matched halls lined with oak doors. I turned left, moving my spurs along the white, sheep-wool imitation. I heard a group laugh from outside. There must have been a window nearby. I noticed one of the doors along the left wall was open and moving up to it I saw the foot of a white bed. I pushed the heavy door, convinced that the spirit of the house had flown outside and I was alone.

The bedroom was empty. And spare. A guest room. I walked in anyway, pretending it was mine and I renowned. My spurs would hang well on the rouge walls. The contrast of those walls with the gold curtains alone felt dated. I touched them, the gold thread woven with a white that didn't appear at a distance.

I pulled the curtains back and squinted at the sun. There, resolving itself, were Corinna's yard and pool. I was standing in the blue house I used to watch when I floated on my back.

I left the empty room without closing the curtains and moved down the corridor toward the shut door at the opposite end of the hall. Why hadn't I noticed how silver the knob was? Next to it, opening it, the knob was like one of Corinna's dad's Hindu things, overlapping ornamentation, lots of empty space. I turned it slowly, pushing gently so there wouldn't be a click.

He was there and not there. Asleep with his mouth open on a green leather sofa—a dead-match for my red one—Jodoin looked only a little more than half alive. The white pallor of his sleeping face made a day's worth of stubble stand out darkly. What looked like a joint balanced unlit in his hand. I sent him a quiet *okay* for sleeping away from his party. I wasn't there either. And Paul was right about how bad he looked. It wasn't age, he was ill. Behind and around the sofa, bookcases stretched from floor to ceiling. Unlike Corinna's dad's old shelves these didn't have the feel of an attic, but of a working kitchen. There was no dust. Between two of the cases, tucked into a corner by the window, sat a cluttered desk. He wrote here. He wrote. Here. I moved quietly across the red and richer-red swirled carpet and touched some of the paper.

*A lean time, no war…*

"Charlie! Hey, that's Charlie's stuff!" Paul's voice? Here? I turned to see him and David in the doorway, coasting into the room. David held an uncorked bottle of Calvados and two glasses of ice. I heard the paper crinkle in my fist, stuffed it into my pocket.

"I didn't see he was here!" I said. "Sleeping?" At which moment Charles Jodoin sat up on the sofa and opened wide blue eyes onto me. He couldn't have been asleep. It's only that he hadn't heard me come in.

"It isn't finished yet," he said. I realized he was looking at me, talking about the paper.

I felt my feet cross to the sofa. I reached into my pocket, the way I had five times a day, rehearsing the moment in my head. I pulled out the Zodiaks. Automatically, I walked forward, blurred with adrenalin.

"Smoke?"

He didn't look down at the packet, but kept his eyes on mine. Angling his head to one side in a way I understood, smiling, he said, "Please," and extended the half inch of a joint. Before I could accept it and start talking, tell him I liked his poetry, that I was a writer too, Paul broke in. "Charlie! David and I were just talking about me doing you guys a favor and looking after this place."

"There you are!" Star marched through the door and straight toward me. "What are you doing with the famous poet?"

"Famous?" Jodoin turned his head to take in the active side of the room and instantly held them in place. I knew already how his blue eyes could fix people and, free of them for a second, I put the ball of crumpled paper on his desk.

"Corinna had a headache and went home," she

said, turning and looking toward Paul. An old woman dressed entirely in pink came into the room behind Star. She was followed by a couple of fortyish men in polo shirts and a painfully thin woman in black shorts and a t-shirt that said *The Other Rhode Island* in 70s swishes.

"So this is where the party is!" *Rhode Island* said, and picked me to smile at, unable even for a second to fill her eyes with the kind of smile Jodoin had cold.

I drifted to the books. None of the stuff I liked was there, but there was lots of Pope, books on gardening. I looked for what felt like an extended time, eventually finding the same copy of Cavafy Corinna's dad used to have. I sat in Jodoin's writing chair pretending to read it, too scared to turn around and read the unfinished desk. *Waiting for the Barbarians*. I saw the tides in the room shift and move; at one point I crossed it to fill my empty glass with some of Paul's Calvados. It took him a long minute to notice me, but he smiled while he poured it, then he turned back to David and Charles. Charles was listening to a long joke getting told by a precise woman in a short skirt and a summer top.

"And the gentleman says, *It happens in the future*." Voices from the lawn outside entered the room in lazy gusts. I felt like an oddity in heavy black, sweating lightly in an armchair, smoking with nowhere to ash. I used a lacquered trashcan when I guessed no one was looking. Every time someone I didn't

know approached me—they were older and mon-
eyed—I buried my eyes in Cavafy and wished Bill
were there. Even if we seemed to need the drugs
it was better with the drugs than it was sober else-
where. Only with Corinna, and before Paul, did it
used to be that good.

Star emerged next to me from the room's increas-
ingly expensive perfume. She'd unbuttoned the top
of the black silk shirt and tied the loose ends at her
belly. The skin I could see above her belt looked
soft and white and I laid my hand against it.

"You gonna get me that shirt back?"

"Yeah, you'd like that, wouldn't you?" She looked
at what I was reading long enough to know she
didn't care. "So…" She took in the room again.
"Do you want to go?"

"You don't like that I'm having so much fun?"

"You look miserable, Jack. Come see Mara. She
heals you."

I looked at her small hand on my arm and remembered a time two or three years earlier when
Star had fallen asleep on the beach with her hand
on my chest. It was just as pale as now, with new
silver rings. They were set with stars made out of
red stones.

"I kinda," motioning with my chin for her to lean
down, "want to talk with the poet at some point."

"Why?"

"Well, I'm a poet."

"I thought you were a playwright. You haven't
even finished a play yet."

"They're going…" I half-rolled my eyes meaning lean closer, "going away again, and he's obviously sick and…." I looked at his books. "I want to look at his books, too."

"Well I want to go and you should go with me."

From the sofa Paul looked at us expressionlessly. Jodoin and David were talking across him.

"Because Paul's not happy," she said.

"He's inebriated…sorry, incarcerated, Jesus…" I was about to say, *He's ensconced in the community.* I was a drunk pretending drunk, but not so drunk as…

"Here," she said. She had one of Bill's blue pills.

"I was about to say…"

She softly said, "Swallow it."

I did. Paul was distracted again, turning to listen to either host as they spoke. I decided she was right and stood up, legs sore from the half-hour. Angling myself out so I'd pass the bookcase, I leaned up to slip Cavafy back. Two or three picture books past it I saw *The Recognitions.*

"Listen. Hey, Star, look at this for a second. It's incredible…"

"Wait!" Jodoin shouted from the couch, starting up. Who was I to touch his books? I hadn't even read it through.

He sprang up birdlike, meaning reptilian plus beauty. His blue eyes made the way he snatched the book seem cordial.

"My favorite book!" As though he'd found it in some old trunk.

I was small again, near to vanishing. I said, "That first paragraph, right?"

He looked both at and past me. "Everything you'll experience is covered in here. How old are you?"

For a small man, his presence seemed big to me. I wondered at how Paul could find the courage to try to sell lawnmowers to such a man.

"I'm twenty."

"Then now is when you have to read this. Who are you reading now? Who's your favorite?"

This was exactly the conversation I wanted to have with Charles Jodoin. I was *some young man*, but that was just as well. It was as though Corinna slid Paul's ring off her finger and fell into my arms.

"Well, you. I read your new one, *Windows,* the other day…"

He nodded. "*Windows* was an interesting book."

I couldn't stop now. I quoted him, "Each year, the world pours through more glass, less thoroughly…" I faltered, skipped. "Omnipresent windows take in murky pools…"

He smiled and said "Stop." *The Other Rhode Island* stood next to me where Star had been.

"But I loved that…" I grabbed onto the only real thought that had rolled into my head when I'd read it. "You trapped yourself in pictures seen through little windows, identified those windows, and didn't go any further…"

"If an artist is lucky," he rolled out, "he will be granted knowledge of the world commensurate with his talent. Look at Tolstoy—all that talent had to have something to wrestle with, so he took on the universe…." He extracted a pack of Marlboros from his pocket and lit one.

"Well!" I said, deciding to kiss ass. "Your talent…"

"Me?" He touched his chest. "Why, I have a modest talent, I suppose." He sipped his drink. "A small, well-furnished room."

*The Other Rhode Island* smiled, in the know. "Zahra's still angry with you."

"…letters in the paper…"

"Or that other one…" she said, real red on her cheeks, "about the fucking."

He smirked. I could see the fuzz of a perfect dope and drink set on his lines.

"Which?"

"Ah, ha!" A shot with all her lungs.

"You laugh at me…"

Why did I already feel the room turning? The way we set memories. Or did I know without thinking?

"…but I stayed in that room this spring. I know about the pool next door. All that fucking going on."

Paul smiled cautiously. He wouldn't know the poem, but he knew his own pool. He knew what Jodoin liked watching. Hell, maybe he'd give him more.

"The one about her husband leaving, the salesman, and the other one fucks her."

The wet sound of *fucks* was all I could catch before my head hit the floor and my cheek pressed the carpet. Someone must have grabbed Paul because I had a good second to register the pound in my head. I rolled and scooted under someone's legs in blue jeans, pressed myself against the built-in bookshelves. I used them to hoist up and take it in. Paul shrugged out of whoever held him for a second and lunged back at me head-first. I instinctively threw my arms out and I had enough thought to grab his shoulders, try to push him off. In half a beat David came up behind Paul and smacked the side of his head while kicking a heel at the back of his knee.

Paul caught his head on the corner of the writing desk when he fell, landing on the carpet like a bundle. I found myself pulling his head onto my lap, his eyes glassy, petting his hair. David knelt as though this were the hundredth time to check Paul's wrist and eyes. I fixed on the moles on his neck.

"Get out!" he told me.

"What the fuck were you talking about?" I meant to ask Jodoin but I asked David because he was close.

He softened a little seeing how I petted Paul's temples but he still said, "Get out."

But Paul was kicking now. He leaned up out of my hands quick and shouted, "Liar!"

"Come here," I said and tried to pull Paul down from under his arms. He turned and swung out at me. David was there, standing up, and he grabbed Paul's right arm and wrenched it around his back.

Paralyzed, Paul turned his eyes on me. They were drunk like I'd see any night, but hard too.

"What did you say that for, Charlie?" I shouted.

Jodoin had his arm around *The Oher Rhode Island* for no reason I could see. No one swung at her.

"Tell him!" I shouted. "It wasn't fucking! You have a responsibility!"

David reached his free hand to lash out at me but Paul lurched forward with a fist — the whole room seemed to back up — and David had to use that hand to hook Paul's arm back again.

I moved toward Jodoin and David jerked up, surged toward me with his hand out. Paul wrapped a new freed arm around David's neck, pulled him back down. Paul was screaming now.

"What!" I shouted at Charles Jodoin, "What!" I must have looked more than angry because someone was pulling my shoulders back. I cast out of those hands enough to jump at Charles Jodoin. I missed and only pulled him down by the legs.

I'd knocked him to the floor. Paul was shouting *Believer.* Everyone was shouting. Star wasn't anywhere.

Jodoin leaned his head up from the floor. In the second before I lost track, felt a foot on the back of my head he surprised me by understanding everything, knowing what I expected to hear, predicting it before I asked.

"No! No! I meant the boy with red hair."

# The Lakes of the Enchanted North

BILL WAS PALE IN THE LIGHTS WE PASSED ON OUR way back to Rt. 2 in Concord. His eyes closed, head lolling on the seat-back. He woke up when I parked just past the 126 intersection as deep as I could on the road bank. The car slowed and stopped in the near total dark, tires crunching old leaves and snow crust.

"I want to wait here," he said.

"Why?"

"Because it wasn't me who left the typewriter in the snow."

I took the cigarette pack out of my pocket and found there weren't any left. I crumpled and tossed it in the back.

"I could use the help, Bill…"

From still to moving in a second he snapped the door open and was out, walking along the road to the pond's front gate.

"Hold up!" I opened the arm rest, fished around for the flashlight. Finally laying my hand around it I scrambled out of the car, locked it, and ran in the direction where I'd seen Bill disappear.

"Bill!" I whispered loud. "Here!" I turned the

flashlight straight on his pissed-off face as we entered the woods. It was colder than two hours ago when we'd left and I was jittery from exhaustion.

I kept the light on the ground, not wanting to alert anyone. We were loud through the leaves, so the light may not have mattered.

"Talk to me," I said. "I feel bad enough about your visit. This was going to be the weekend we wrote the big play."

The trampled brush was wide enough to seem like a path. To the extent I thought about it, I guessed if we just kept walking in as straight a line as possible we'd eventually reach the pond. It was a big pond and there wasn't much wood between it and the road.

"I'll call you," I said, "or maybe I can just go ahead and write the first scene on my own and I'll mail it to you or something, and you can do whatever you like with it."

Bill kept walking a foot or two ahead of me. I was careful to keep the light in front of his feet, but it looked as though he'd walk on without it. The moon was gibbous, *wafer white*. I had to stop thinking like bad poetry. Bad, pseudo-religious poetry. Nothing religious about me. I managed to fuck up a pilgrimage. The snot in my nose had frozen pretty solid by then. I didn't have anywhere else to wipe it so I used my sleeve.

"Tell me," I asked, "about your Long Island girl. That'll cheer you up. You said you were going to her place in the afternoons. That her mom's not home. Have you met her mom?

"Wait," I said, "Stop. Fuck, my feet are frozen solid. Fuck, it hurts." Spurs. "So. Indians. I like your idea about them. Say we take her off the train. What if she's settled down near some Indian reservation, and she makes friends or something with one of the Indian women there, you know, about her age, and they've led such wildly different lives but as they pursue it, they find that their lives have all these odd similarities. That they lived almost the same life. And that…" My mind, after trying all day, only started working now that there was almost no chance Bill was listening. "You know, at first the Indian is resentful of the white woman's — or fuck, make her a black woman, complicate it — but anyway she's resentful of her position or status, you know, not having had to grow up on a reservation filled with alcoholic Indians and burned out cars…"

"Where's the action?" Bill asked colorlessly.

"Well, that's where you come in."

"So I write the play?"

"Well, we'll go back and forth."

"Where's the action, Jack. You need action." He turned and stared at me. I put the light up to his face for a second until I realized I shouldn't. Then I just shut it off since we weren't moving anymore.

"Drama," he said coldly, "is about fucking or fighting. Where's that?"

"Okay!" I said. "Fuck! I don't know. Don't be confrontational!"

"I'm out here in the cold!" he said. "I'm miles from…"

"You came up here," I said. "To the Lakes of the Enchanted North to write a play. Now we're cold and we're in the dark and we have no idea…look at us Bill, we have no idea where we are! Which is… typical of the way we've been operating." I smiled. "And we're finally getting to it. Overture was getting fucked up. Now we're literally fucked up. We've been fucked. The day has fucked us."

He was laughing, even if it sounded soft. My eyes had adjusted enough to see his dark shape sink against a tree. My gut was moving and I started laughing too. We kept on like that for awhile. I took my boots off with trouble and cupped my bare toes—we'd been too drunk for me to think of socks. My back against a tree, wet leaves underneath me, I unclipped my spurs and dropped them into my pocket. The cheap metal probably didn't conduct that much cold anyway. The real fault was with the cheap leather.

"She wanted to get together this weekend but I said no, I have to work on a play with Jack. And I told her about you and she said 'You just get fucked up with Jack.'"

"Well, fuck her. We're making art. We're at the center of American…the heart of America, which isn't the Midwest because we stole that from the Indians, as you say, but we're right where one man said fuck it, fuck them all. Have you read *Civil Disobedience*?"

"Don't try to tell me you have."

"Well I saw the title. I know he was in jail."

"Let's go back to the car," Bill said.

"No, let's find…here, I'll give you the keys, you can go back if you like."

We didn't move for a while. I began to make out the shapes of the trees behind the one Bill slumped against. The cold felt good for a minute, the way cold can.

"Alright," I said, aware that waking life finds its own temporal rules and that the time to talk about the play had passed. "You want drama, let's say the American girl is married."

"Indians are Americans. Fuck 'em."

"Whatever, you know what I mean." I pulled on my stiff boots. "And it emerges that, you know, people aren't that different, culture to culture. Our narrator learns…"

"It's a play, there's no narrator." Bill was shifting. Now that my eyes were adjusted I saw what looked like a break in the trees not far ahead. We'd been sitting not feet from the railroad tracks. The pond had to be spitting close.

"Whatever, she learns that despite…"

"Where's the drama?" My eyes adjusted enough to see Bill's pale face as dark.

"I'm going back to the car," he said. "Give me the flashlight. It's just a typewriter. It'll be here in the morning."

"First," I said, standing, shivering, "drama. I'll… how about…do you absolutely need some? Okay.

How about this…the reservation girl has a husband and the non-reservation girl falls in love with him. She heard the other girl's stories about Crazy Horse and she thinks the guy's Crazy Horse. And even though they're friends, and good, absolute friends, she's trying to fuck what's her name's husband. And…" Write what you know. "Because she thinks she'll leave herself that way, be part Native American somehow, like she can leave herself. So sex is a metaphor. I mean, it's a metaphor, but she's still trying to fuck him."

"Like you're…" Bill stopped himself hard. We'd reached the pond. All I could see was a few yards of water lapping the dirt. No vista.

"Like I'm trying to fuck your high school girlfriend?" I threw it out.

"This is *my life*." Bill grabbed my lapels, fumbling once because of the dark. I grabbed him back, adrenalin awake. "This isn't *material*."

"Why do you… I can see the way you look when I talk. It's my life too. It's as much my life now."

"Oh? Why?" Bill demanded. "Have you fucked her?"

"The whole world," I shouted, "can't be your life!" I pushed him off and he stayed off. He knew it was a bad idea to snap. He knew we were standing in the cold.

"Go that way," he commanded, wresting the conversation back to his directorial mien. "I'll go this way. Whoever finds the typewriter keeps it."

Why argue with a good idea? I turned and walked

up my half of the path. My half wound through what, based on our afternoon, I thought of as the back way.

Nothing was familiar in the dark. All of the nature we'd seen stayed hidden and only the dark was there, world reduced to the size of the light from the flashlight. The tips of my boots.

I'd been walking a few minutes in the snow, pointing the light at the near and far edges of the path, just starting to feel alone and adventurous when I realized that there was only one flashlight and it was in my numb hand.

I didn't want Bill walking without one. I didn't like the idea of finding he'd stumbled or, more likely, wandered off the path. I thought about keeping on plodding but realizing I'd probably only gone a little way I turned around and started moving in the direction I'd come from. Since I had the light I figured I could run and I ran. It helped to warm me up anyway.

"Bill!" I shouted, not caring for a second if we were overheard by some other creature. I quickly passed the spot I knew we'd parted at. I kept walking and, since I had the flashlight, running.

# Driver

I opened the door of Corinna's room onto the thumbed row of romance novels and smaller row of the untouched books — poetry, short stories I'd given her. I could smell the scent of her shampoo. Like someone who's waited for something to happen for a long time and, when it finally does, is made strong by it, I pushed through her room and downstairs to the backyard. The afternoon sun made me feel how deep drunk I was. I'd expected huge swaths of time to have passed since I left Jodoin's party, but the light still fell brightly on the water. I heard Star come through the screen door behind me. The yard was empty.

"Where are they?"

"They're not here," she said. It sounded like she was guessing.

"We don't…" I was so gathered with adrenalin my mind worked too fast, "actually know she's not here. She said she didn't feel well, right?"

I looked at Star, her pink, exaggerated mouth, smart eyes.

"I saw him."

"Okay. Where?" It felt as though I were speeding.

Thinking back to the blue pill, I remembered I was.

"We should go back and check on Paul."

"Fuck…where?"

She drew back. Yelling at Star was the worst way to do this.

"Please."

"I told him I wouldn't tell you."

"Well you told me now."

"I just ran into him. Before I came…"

"Yeah, I guessed. Where is he?"

"I don't know."

One thing Star can't do is lie.

"Star." I tried to hold her eyes.

"Promise you won't go there."

Fingers crossed.

"They're on the boat."

"I can't believe she does this when he's at the… when Paul's home. When they were at a party…"

"Jack!" She said, "Come on, Jack. She lets you feel her up while he's in the other room!"

We both walked through the house and out. I didn't know it then, but I wouldn't be back. I said a perfunctory goodbye to the library and the kitchen. I'd only care later.

I didn't question it when Star climbed into the car next to me. She put her hand on my arm as I started the car. I turned and kissed her full on the mouth. She kissed me back like she'd been waiting for it. The caution we'd kept was gone. Corinna was out of the way. Corinna who never cared was out of the way. I was Star's alone for a while and she knew it. There was a little fuzz on her upper lip but I liked it, kissed it. She kissed out with her lower lip and we were back and forth like that, pulling in close. I touched her chin and she stopped. I hadn't wanted her to, so I took my hand away and she kissed me as hard as before. We pressed our open mouths together, reached as far as we could.

"It'll take me twenty minutes," I said, pulling back, "then we'll go to Mara's. Or wherever you want to go."

"He'll know I told you."

"Star," I said, "I haven't talked to him in six months."

"I know. He said you weren't friends anymore."

Paul appeared in the rearview, with a pristine Panama hat in his hand and a red eye already turning purple.

"No harm!" I said, clicking open the door, holding my arms out, palms out. "Truce."

He stopped where he was, looked out at me, eyes full of everything that just happened. I'd taken the Adderall but Paul looked as pulled as a string in those long pieces he liked where the violinists start plucking.

"Where are they?"

"Come with me."

He shook his head, shouted, "Where are they!"

I heard Star shout, "Stop it Paul!" But she didn't emerge. I wished I was back in the car.

"Are they upstairs? Are they on the boat?" he asked, voice choked.

"Star told me, she saw him, but don't ask her about it, don't…"

"Tell the pussy to get in!" Star yelled from inside the car. I turned around to see her head hanging out of the door. I'd left the driver's door open and two cars were lined up to pass this narrow road on the path, I guessed, to the main route along the bay.

"Go," I gestured widely, "it's wide enough."

They kept honking. With a big Fuck You show, I walked a few steps back to the car and, checking for Star's fingers, slammed the door. They sailed past slow enough for me to recognize *The Other Rhode Island* in one car and what was probably Star's old teacher in another.

The convenience store whose proprietor took offense over *Windows* stood at the end of the street.

*the soda stand, whose owner TAKES ME IN*
*With eyes alone, unshattered stare*

And in front of me was no one. Paul had disappeared. I touched my sore eye, told myself that Paul and I had been going through the motions since Corinna… I climbed back into the car and started driving toward the main route to the harbor.

In silence, Star and I passed the sleeping white ships, the long stretches, breakwaters. I watched every shadow on the darkening road.

"Well, that's that," I said. "Throw him away. I mean I already threw him away…"

"If I thought it would do any good I'd tell you to

turn the car around and…"

"Why…fuck…"

Star sighed. "She said you're not fun for her because you just lie around and read all day. You're just like her."

"And Bill isn't?"

"Bill fucks actresses in New York."

"He reads."

"Yeah, but it's like all you do."

"That's not all I do! I write…"

"No you don't."

"I will. Anyway, I'm just like Bill."

"No, Jack, you're not. You try to be just like Bill."

"So why do you like me then? Honestly, I don't know why anyone does or doesn't. Because I'm just like them, I guess. Or not. I don't know why anybody wants to fuck anybody. Why did I want to fuck Corinna anyway. Fuck. Fuck. Sorry. Like, on a practical level, of course it wouldn't work. We're too…I know that. I knew that. And that made me angry too. Because she's so beautiful, or…we have…we have something…"

"You just want to be Bill," Star said. If our trip to the harbor pissed her off a little, my monologue finished her patience. "You want to, like, eat Bill. You clearly don't care about Paul."

"Paul," I stopped her, angry, "is like my brother." And I could let him go.

I parked the car neatly in the empty lot. Angry, even with the parking lot, I slammed the door like cannon fire, taste of metal in my mouth. Star said she would wait there and I said alright. It had grown dark by now, but I could make out the silhouette of the docked boat in its berth, still as the ships they sold in paintings down the street.

I crossed the lot in the windless summer heat and jogged up to the cruiser. They weren't on deck, and wouldn't be anyway. I pulled my feet out of my long boots on the middle of the dock and left them off to the side. I hadn't landed a hit in all the fighting and I was ready to with my tight hands. In the back of my mind, this was a cacophonous misunderstanding. Jodoin had mistaken Bill, or he was high and confused. Bill was really there to talk with Corinna about how to get back in touch with me, what that might entail. Climbing gingerly onto the deck, trying not to shake the hull, I felt as though he should be part of this, but with me, buoying me. My eyes pricked and the dark sky looked purple. I saw colors, felt naked. Creeping, I approached the hatch and listened for voices. With the same faculty that warns of being watched, I knew I wasn't alone on the boat. I crept my head around the side of the hatch but there was nothing yet, just the couple of feet of red carpet you could see from there.

When I was small, I used to creep into my parents' room at night. Their smell hit first, like tired breath and shoe leather, motes of Mom's perfume. In the dark, I couldn't tell one from another. There was no traffic, and I measured my breathing in sips. That's what this felt like.

I eased a wet sock foot onto the ladder, then,

cautiously, I was standing there. I lowered my head as much as I could to see down and decided it wouldn't work, I'd have to keep crawling head first. I stood up carefully and lowered myself on the heels of my hands. There was a human sound from the belly of the boat. I couldn't tell what it was exactly but I knew what it was about. My fingers wrapped the varnished molding. Incautiously, I sunk my head down far enough that I could take in the whole cabin.

They held each other. Corinna, feet braced on the floor, undressed but for her raised shirt and his hand raising it higher, seemed almost to be falling off the couch. She faced him, her back to me. With his right hand, he cupped her ass and pulled her onto his lap. His left hand disappeared. I guessed he must be holding her breast as they kissed.

Her hand was on his lap, she seemed to be fumbling, caught up. I wasn't self-conscious anymore, understanding that they wouldn't be looking up to the hatch. Even though I could have reached them with a few more steps. I felt myself bizarrely one with Bill. I knew what she felt like, knew how she tasted in my mouth.

I crept back up to the dock and collected my boots. Star knew.

"Let's go to Mara's party," I said.

"Are you sure?"

The lights of a new car signaled in as we pulled out of the lot. It was Paul's hatchback.

# Coming Down

STAR DIRECTED THE CAR THROUGH THE DARK.
I tried to tamp my jittering down, but it was there.
All my fingers jumped on the wheel. I had to for-
mulate my words in a small space toward the front
of my mouth, holding back my spit, shoulders tight.

Once, Bill and I had tried to talk a forty-year-old
woman, drunk, back to his dorm. She was trying to
quit drinking, she said, and each time we proposed
*Let's go*, she went back for another. We were seven-
teen years old in a West 4th Street bar, and I felt like
I might jump out of my skin.

I felt that way now.

"Where am I turning?"

"Just like you're going to the Fort. You've never
gone to the Fort?"

The Fort turned out to be a series of low, varie-
gated hills strung with hedgerows. I remembered
that a fort could mean a bare foundation on a
green. So the picture in my head hadn't been any
good. *Mara's Fort* quit feeling solid, turned green
and spread.

"Turn left here. No, just past the headlights,
there."

I pulled the car onto the side of a hill. What had seemed like a lake through the dark turned into a low sweep of grass. There were seven or eight tents set up near its edge, most of them clustered together but a few set off and apart.

I felt sick to my gut walking over the dirt and stones of the road away from the car. I wasn't morally allowed that nausea and no one knew that better than Star. Even then, when I least wanted to, I had to play cool. If I was too broken up, got drunk too fast, or flashed angry, whatever she and I had been simmering these last months would dissipate. I'd be alone.

So I put my hand around her, felt her arm under the thin silk of her shirt. I rolled my fingers down to her hand and took it as she raised it up to her belly. I pulled her against me from behind and touched her breasts, unbuttoning the top of her shirt.

She turned around to kiss me but she pulled back as soon as we'd tensed, kissed, and let go.

"We can go into Mara's tent tonight," she said.

"Okay. Does Mara…?"

"No. She lets me use her tent. I've done it before."

My eyes adjusted to the dark in time to see Star being bashful.

"Come on down and meet her."

"I didn't…Wait! Star!…do they have…"

"There'll be beer."

As we lowered ourselves hand in hand down the hill, I thought about all those teenage evenings with

Bill when we'd stayed up hours after the liquor was gone. He and I would drive out to a lake or park in false dawn, new moon, Pleiades. We'd laugh about how we wanted to transcend the mundane world of people who looked at their shoes all day. We would stare at whatever we'd come to see, hoping it would lift us, laugh ourselves sick about how it never did.

A couple of kids were piling up what looked like prep for a bonfire. What struck me was how they seemed to have brought it all along with them, unwrapping big sticks from rolled sheets.

"All these guys," Star smiled, "are real. That's why I like them. They're not all fake like Paul and Corinna, or you sometimes."

"They're just as scared of being middling," I muttered. "They've just chosen a different path to wisdom."

She made as if not to hear me as we reached the base of the hill and dropped hands. I put my arm around her, tucked her into my side as we walked. Her legs were shorter, though, and I hadn't managed to correct for that by the time we reached the edge of the woodpile.

The boys smiled at Star and the girls hugged her. The girls were dressed like a scavenger hunt authority told them they had an hour to impersonate flappers. The boys had short hair and, despite the heat, gas station jerseys.

I kicked a couple of logs into place. Or what I thought was in place. One of the boys with bottle-black hair looked at me as though he wondered what the hell I was doing there. Star introduced me to the girls from over her shoulder.

"That's Jack." It was clear she'd told them about me because one or two of them smiled, knowingly.

A tall girl with what looked like naturally blond hair walked up to the group. She wore a sleeveless white tee shirt and lots of sliver necklaces. "I like your cowboy hat." I realized I'd been holding it. I put it on. She smiled a beat slow.

"But you don't need it," she said, studying me. "You're just a pretty boy aren't you? That's your secret."

"Let's keep that between you and me," I said.

She looked as if what I'd said had put her off. I hadn't meant it to, but I wasn't in my right mind. She moved off and I was left standing with Star and the fire makers.

I wanted her attention. "Star!"

Star looked over her shoulder. One of her friends, a skinny boy in a long coat with shiny buttons, looked up at me as though he was confused about why I wasn't someone else.

"Do you want…Star! Do you want a drink, or…?"

"I'll get something in a second," Star said, turning back to her friends. She must have been telling them about what had happened tonight. I didn't want to hear about it, even if it was the only thing in my head.

"I'm going for a drink, okay?"

I moved off toward the biggest cluster of tents.

The first one I entered turned out to be empty except for an unopened bottle of something called pear wine. It would have been useless if it wasn't a screw top. It was, though, and I succeeded in opening it. It wasn't bad. It was too sweet to drink in big gulps but I would have drunk anything in gulps, so there was no preventing it.

They were trying to set fire to the wood now. The small lights from their Zippos didn't make the dark field seem any brighter or easier to take in, it just illuminated their round faces, pulled them out of the big blackness. Standing there, finishing some pear wine, watching them fuck it up, I grew aware of voices from a tent maybe twenty feet off. Noticing that it was gradually filling with people I walked over and poked my head between the open flaps. Three or four flashlights faced up from the ground at the center of an informal circle. The white of the tent roof cast a hard glow down as the group passed a long purple bong around. I sat down next to a fortyish man in a short-sleeved button-down shirt with gold-sewn fish leaping up the left side.

"So," I said, taking a long hit I felt to the bottom of my lungs, passing it on, "how do you know Mara, or…?"

Something about how clipped and unselfconscious his gestures seemed made me think he wasn't native. The sound of his voice validated my guess, South American.

"Mara is my angel!"

"Oh?"

"Who are you?" A smile in his voice.

"Jack. Jack Ahern. I know Star."

"Star is a small girl? She has a star here?" He pointed to his neck.

"Yeah. I'm a Jack. Jack up my sleeve."

He nodded slow. I couldn't gauge whatever he mouthed now because I was swaying like I was on a boat in a storm. For a few minutes at a time I could enter the world and perform in it, but the waves kept on. Even though each wave brought the same tightness in my chest, the same blur in my head, they rolled differently. My mind stopped, turned, and fixed on the picture of Bill and Corinna. I couldn't separate them, her rolling off his body. Since that night in Concord, I kept thinking I'd get a letter or a phone call, though I hadn't tried to be in touch. After tonight, I wouldn't take the call.

"Are you going to make love to that thing or smoke it?"

I realized I'd been waiting with the mouthpiece on my lips, but I hadn't lit it. I didn't. I passed it along to a plump girl in a hot pink top. I stood up and walked into the warm air.

There was more smoke than fire coming up from the high jumble of sticks but it looked like it was going to catch. With only a tacky drop or two left in the pear wine bottle I wandered in the direction of the music coming from the farthest tent.

Most of the light inside was cast by the green and red glow on the big, battery-fueled stereo. A couple of girls in black shuffled through a stack of CDs.

One of them wanted to play David Bowie and the other tried to ease her into something faster.

"Oh, yeah, he's great. How about this? Or like maybe Bowie, sure, but more his new stuff. I want to dance, don't you? There's nothing on here but how about…"

"Have you got any Leonard Cohen?"

They pretended not to hear me, kept fumbling.

"Hi, Jack."

The voice was a little familiar. Turning around, I saw the girl who'd asked about my cowboy hat by the bonfire. She smiled when I turned, she pushed her shoulders back.

"Star told me who you were. I should have known you'd be moping off by yourself."

She chewed her gum at me, made a face when she smacked it.

"Do you like that? I hate this gum. I want to start smoking and drinking, so." She showed off the blunt and the bottle of red wine in her hands.

Only a little awkwardly, I held my palm underneath her mouth. She spat the gum into it, wiping her lip with her thumb.

"Thanks. Let's go bury it in the woods." She urged her chin up.

I looked at the wine.

"Are you sharing?"

"I'm sharing everything," she said, taking a drag of her blunt, touching her lips to mine. I took it in lightly and so there was only a ghost of smoke when I exhaled. Chapped, like Star had said about her lips.

"We're adventurers tonight?" I asked, looking off to the dark.

"I'm coming down," she said. "I'm easing back."

"Coming down from what?"

She smiled huge. We walked over the dark field. Walking with her felt good. I blamed the pear wine. There was mist at the treeline shading the green. The sky when I looked up was wet, starless. What sounded like a fight came out at us in hollers from the bonfire but she didn't turn around.

"Don't you need to go take charge?" I asked. "Start spitting cusses?"

"I don't know these people," she said, looking more intently at the woods that seemed suddenly reachable, as opposed to the mythical treeline you could see from the fire. We walked wordlessly uphill until the line of brush thinned as we neared it.

"Are we going to get lost?"

She handed me the bottle, lowered herself against the base of what may have been an old stone wall or raised foundation. I sat across from her, leaning my back against an oak.

"We used to visit forts," I said, "like this, when I was a kid. My dad was in Vietnam and his dad was in Germany so…I was just bored the whole time."

I opened my hand so she could see her still wet gum and dropped it into a cluster of bushes. Instinct made me wonder if Mara's comfortable and easy nature might be like a knife, our walk to the woods the cool, smooth side. Still.

"Star…" she was delicate, "told me about to-night. But what I want to know is what's the deal with Star?"

"Please," I said, looking in her eyes. "I've had a long day." The fire must have been going by then because I smelled the smoke.

"Well the day's not over, Jack."

"Who are all those people?" I asked. "I grew up here and I don't know them. There can't be some, I don't know. A *scene.* I know all kinds of people. I went to high school here."

"You don't know anyone," she said. "Who are you kidding? You've spent the whole year in the doorway of Corinna's bedroom."

"I like to watch."

"Apparently."

"You were rude to me," I changed my tack, "by the fire."

"I didn't know who you were. A cowboy hat and you come with Star but I didn't know. Yeah, Star said, that's Jack, but why not just get you alone?"

With anyone else I would have maybe moved a little closer. But with her I stayed immobile. I liked how her eyes reflected firelight while they took me in. Her talk, the presence of someone like her, was all that held me back from free fall.

"You probably can't see it," she said, "but Star got hit harder by the whole marriage thing than you did. She was like Corinna's little sister, you know."

"Now she's yours."

"Yeah," she said, "but she wants to be yours."

I heard the drag of what was probably music coming loud from the tents. I guessed they were dancing.

"So if she can't be Corinna's little sister she wants to be my little sister?"

Her big eyes rolled and I moved my hand, *Come here.*

"Let's go closer down," she said, "I want to watch what's going on now."

She stood up, brushed her shirt off, and I put my hand on her shoulder to guide her down the hill again. As we lowered ourselves she wrapped her arm around my waist. I pulled her close, sniffed the top of her head. Her perfume, or shampoo, or however the way her head smelled the way it did wasn't like Corinna's. It was unlike enough that I felt drugged walking back to the tents.

There were ships moored at the breakwaters. The War of Independence monument stood in the distance like a buried lighthouse. Our job was to unmoor all the boats before the tide rose higher, making sure they were full of at least four hands before they let go.

"There's someone still stuck in one of these!" An old woman, her leg twisted, sprawled on the floor, shouting in pain and staring at me with abandoned eyes. The chorus hollered *Let her go.* I knew that Corinna and Star and David were there but whenever I turned around all I saw was sharp, wet rocks. It's because I wasn't keen enough to find them. My eyes were bad.

The old woman was really *The Other Rhode Island* dressed forty years out of date.

*You have to go with her, Jack.*

Her eyes didn't stop and they called me in.

So I jumped in the water to escape the dream, felt it welling up around me.

Then light from the cabin skylight, the sound of hard rain.

The canvas of the tent roof beat so steadily I didn't hear it for what it was until I felt awake enough to open my eyes.

I felt someone alongside me, moving underneath my arm.

"Mara?"

"Jack." It was Star. I instinctively smoothed her hair. I always woke up ready when I felt hungover. She was lifting my shirt up, kissing my chest.

I arched against her. Her small hand rubbed over the black jeans I still wore. I pulled them unbuttoned and in a second she was already on top of me and we were moving hard and wet against each other. I loosened the knot on her borrowed shirt. I was sore all over and my throat felt dry as cloth. All I could do was lie there, reaching up to smooth her hair. She'd bite the heel of my hand. She beat herself hard up and down on top of me, writhing, reaching into herself and contracting. Then once more and more rough.

I'd reached for a mental image of Corinna at the

moment I'd cum each time for years. I reached for Mara instead and she filled my mind. Then her face broke up and Star stopped pulsing, although she stayed on top of me, kept me inside. She smiled wet eyes, searching, happily.

I ran my hands down her soft arms and laughed, rolling my head back, watching her. She laughed back and we stayed like that, soaked from last night's toxins.

"Mara tucked you in," she told me a little later, her face close, her arms folded on my chest. "You were gone, Jack, you'd had it. By the time you guys made it back to the fire no one could understand what you were saying. Thank god she tucked you in. You would have wandered into the forest, woken up with some possum."

I smiled because I was thinking.

"We're in Mara's tent?"

"She said you kept telling her not to hold your arms back."

I tried to appear devilish but it was impossible. "Was I being untoward?"

"Yeah, you were. She thought it was funny."

Star and I traded shirts. I put on the black silk I'd loaned her in the dark ages and walked into the rained-out morning. A few of the boys I'd met last night were stomping, drying, and scattering the charred logs.

"You want some coffee?" one of them asked. I realized he'd been the boy in brass buttons. He wore a flannel shirt now and looked ten years older, maybe because of the stubble on his face.

"Thanks," I said and he handed me a paper cup, filled it from a big metal thermos.

I smelled the steam and watched mist both rise and fall from the field. They were folding their tents.

"It's morning in America," I said.

Buttons moved off. "Be prepared."

# He Plays Her Room

SONYA:     WORDS. (PAUSE) WORDS ARE MAGIC.
           YOU open your mouth and let this
           beast into the world and the fool
           thing eats the world. You open your
           mouth and you just make everything
           hungrier.

Onstage, Sonya wore her hair in braids and nervously fingered her flared skirt. A soft-featured boy sat beside her with a Wyle E. Coyote stick of dynamite and a poised lighter. He wore jeans with rolled cuffs, hair in a messed-up spit-curl. He hadn't lit the dynamite.

Since the last writer's scene ended and Bill's began, the lights were up on Sonya speaking of how she and the boy would leave together, escaping the Indian inside her and the father who abused her (the reason the Indian had appeared in her youth, it seemed, emerging from her anger and fear to totemically protect her). She was pregnant, and how could it be safe to raise the baby with that Indian around? They'd raise it somewhere far away, after her father's house had burned. Hence the dynamite. They'd explode the place and drive off.

Behind Sonya and the boy, in a stand-alone door-frame, loomed a headdressed Pequot warrior with a shell medallion around his neck and his arms marked with tattoos. The Indian was Toby.

Julie leaned toward me and whispered, "Toby's fucking Sonya."

"Oh yeah? How long?"

But she was back to watching.

Sonya: (heated, to Toby) You're just a word, you hear? A word outta skin and bone. But I've got a real person in me now, a real baby that's gonna separate outside of me. And you can't be part of me then! You have to go!

I could feel Bill somewhere in the seats behind me, or out in the foyer or in the tech box. The theater smelled like new dust. I ran through what I might try to say:

Jack: I had to come, Bill. I believe in your work…

Jack: Why did you disappear? Why didn't you call?

Jack: There's horsetrank in my pocket… let's go over there (points offstage at a closet with a cold sink)…we'll have a line and go somewhere real…

Onstage, Sonya and Toby grappled, growling.

They mimed a struggle; they punctuated their swipes with stomps, but since you weren't looking at their feet the stomps stood in for landing blows. Sonya scuffed when she staggered back.

I hadn't seen Bill: not in the park or on the Summer Street Bridge or in one of the corners of the lobby or the seats. I could feel him around, though. The scene was more meaningful with him there.

I hadn't called Corinna since the party. She hadn't called me either. Star left messages I listened to but didn't return. She told me Corinna's house was being sold for good this time, that Corinna and Paul were over, that she was sorry she was being so annoying.

She'd be in school in Boston for another two years. I was beginning my last, unanchored. It sped in my mind while I woke listening to the street, made coffee, came in the shower, walked out into the city. I thought I would have left some mark on the neighborhood, that I'd see the years I'd lived there.

Onstage, Sonya and Toby still fought, half-crouching now and barely sweeping their arms.

Sonya:     (panting) Either you're real or
           everything else is.

Her boyfriend had busied himself debating whether to ignite the dynamite. He lit the spear now and rushed at Toby, pushing him back into the doorframe and killing the stage lights. There was a roar through the audio. The cyclorama lit red and orange and silhouetted Sonya's blur as she ran away from the blaze.

The orange lights went down and we could hear the actors re-shuffling the set into place for the next scene.

"What the fuck just happened?" Julie whispered.

"I think she got away. I think Toby didn't. So maybe she's free of him."

In the next scene—I didn't know who wrote it—a tenured Harvard professor had moved in with a trash-mouth girl from Southie. Sonya played the professor.

Prof:    Why do you roam the house at night? You don't want to sleep? You could have told me you'd be up all night…

The Southie girl wore a wife-beater and had huge eyes, deep-set and dark. It was her who'd played the spit-curled boy.

"Is that the boy from the last scene?"

"Yes," Julie said. "That is the boy."

The professor told her she'd sit up with her, sing to her, tell her stories, anything to get her to fall asleep. But the girl ended up doing most of the talking, going on about how lonesome she'd always been. Against her better judgment the professor climbed into bed with her. Lights down.

I looked into the seats behind me during the scene shift but couldn't locate Bill. The idea of him not being there cleared the color out of the room. Like when I walked back to my car from the boat after Jodoin's party and half of the world I knew snapped away like a sleight of hand.

Or like our walk back from the pond together, no typewriter and a long drive home in silence, Bill slinking out to the train when I lay on the couch and fell asleep — the way I felt on waking with The Apartment empty, no typewriter left.

Then there was a short scene from *The Tempest*, for some reason: Caliban's confrontation with Prospero (*I had peopled else this isle…*), then lights down again. The last scene took place in a hospital where all the verbs and nouns were replaced with profanities. I picked my pink flyer/program off the floor and saw that CB had written it. Also, the girl who played the boy with the spit-curl was named Kat. No bio note about Bill.

Then the show was over and it was time to go into the lobby and find him. I stole a slug from Julie's bottle of Evian and what I thought was water turned to bile in my mouth. I said something like *Excuse me* and got up during the applause and dodged through the seats to the lobby closet with the coldwater sink. Bill wasn't in the lobby and I managed to swallow the sting down. Inside the water closet with the door shut I tried breathing into the sink and choked. I pulled the little packet of horsetrank out of my pocket and emptied it into the drain, then ran my head under the cold tap. My hands were shaking.

I took a bunch of long, slow breaths, inhaling from deep in my belly. I wanted a cigarette so badly I sucked on the palm of my hand.

There was no way to leave but the front door in the lobby and I didn't trust myself to seem alright. I could hear the knob of the door start to move and I stood up straight in time to startle Toby. He wore a bunched black sweater and still had zags of red war paint on his face.

"Who's in here?" he said, smiling and looking past me.

I told him it was just me. That I was just leaving.

"I'm going to take some of this off," he said, calmly gesturing at his face, "then we're going to take a walk and have a drink."

I told him I'd see him then, and stepped into the crowded lobby. Sonya was still in her bathrobe from the second-to-last scene, open to reveal flesh-colored tights. The dancer who'd played Ariel was heading outdoors with a cigarette between her lips. A few well-wishers in overcoats mingled, hugged the actors they'd come to see.

None of the lobby people looked like Bill, but I paused on each to be sure, then I scanned carefully from one end to the other.

Toby had come out of the water closet by then.

"Toby! Did Bill come? To see his play?"

"Bill?"

"This stuff," I said, reaching my hand up to wipe

a little red paint remaining on Toby's face. I knew he wouldn't flinch and he didn't.

"Bill Brennan." Toby said with recognition.

"Yes," I said.

"No. He said no at the last minute. I tried. I said let's he and you and I go out with the cast, but he pulled out." Toby raised his eyebrows. "Do you want to come out for a drink with us or is everyone going to turn me down?"

I felt my leg go on Toby's word that he'd used my name. Our world had touched the outer world again, our world over. Bill not coming was acknowledgement, if I read it right, the way I wanted to. I kept standing up and looking casual but my whole body was shaking by then. I had to move. Outside the theater was nothing but the blank world. I thought I'd go and talk, as though I were whole in my skin.

Kat, the spit-curl girl, was talking with Julie and Calaban by the door. I walked over and smiled at Julie. Kat's accent sounded Russian.

"...pull off the special bra, throw on the night shirt, and all in the dark..."

"Are you..." I caught her eye and paused the way Bill would, "you were great, by the way, I don't know you from school, right?"

"No, I'm Havahd," she said, doing the school's name New England patrician.

Toby gestured at the doors and we started walking toward them as a group. It was still day outdoors and the sun was bright.

"You actually had me convinced you were a boy," I said.

"I think I look boyish," she said. "That's why Toby cast me, right Toby?"

"No," I said, "that only makes the inner woman all the more clear." I exaggerated my confidence and she saw it was okay.

We crossed the Summer Street Bridge. There were some pylons in the water that may or may not have been an unfinished art project, polished scrap metal emerging in rounded shapes.

"Is that your actual accent?" I said. "It's so funny that you can do Southie so perfectly but then you sound…are you Russian?"

"I'm Croatian Alsatian whatever," she said. "My inner woman is all the world."

"This city is your womb," I said, liking her.

She shook her head. "This city is my child."

Kat followed Toby into the lobby of a bank to get some cash and I half-listened to the others talk while I scanned the city for Bill, still not believing he wasn't there, hurt and giddy. A chance to be Bill without Bill there, misplaying him.

I shook, from hands to feet.

I wanted to walk away and away but stayed there, waited for the bank door to re-open. The crowded streets had cleared out with evening and the sky deepened into '80s blue. I half-expected Bill to turn the corner; I half-expected Corinna along with him. Or Jodoin arm-in-arm with Star. I might live all my life and see them twice more.

How long would Star hold on to the shirt I lent her?

Breathe in.

It's a tall day.

There's a blue wind.

Nothing at sea.

## Acknowledgements

Thanks to Elisa Gabbert and Adam Golaski.

I'm lucky to have had an editor who believed in this book as much as I did, David Schloss, at Miami. To him and to Dana Leonard and Keith Tuma, I owe a real debt.

Also: Jennifer Kristen Olson and Chip Cheek in Boston, Kirsten Lewis in Richmond, Kathleen Rooney in Chicago, and Kevin Caron in Boulder.

And thanks to my family in the East and Midwest.

John Cotter is a founding editor of the online magazine Open Letters Monthly. He was born in Norwich, Connecticut and lives in Jamaica Plain, Massachusetts.

Other titles in the Miami University Press fiction series:

To see our complete catalog of poetry and fiction, please visit www.muohio.edu/mupress.